ERIC CLAPTON

slowhand

INTERVIEWS COURTESY OF ROCK'S BACKPAGES

 ABSTRACT SOUNDS BOOKS LTD

Abstract Sounds Books Ltd

Unit 207, Buspace Studios, Conlan Street, London W10 5AP

www.abstractsoundsbooks.com

© Abstract Sounds Books Ltd 2010

Published by Abstract Sounds Books Ltd

Licensed from Archive Media Publishing Ltd

ISBN: 978-0-9566959-5-6

DVD CREDITS

All film interviews are copyright Archive Media Publishing Ltd

BOOK CREDITS

BOOK PHOTOGRAPHY CREDITS

contents

4 | **ERIC CLAPTON** slowhand

an interview with
ERIC CLAPTON

(RITCHIE YORKE, CIRCUS, 1970)

Eric Clapton started work on his solo album while in Los Angeles with Delaney and Bonnie. He came back to England with the unfinished, unmixed tapes and went to work with Bill Halverson, the well-known engineer who recently split Wally Heider's scene and went solo himself. Everyone was wondering what Eric was planning. Was he going to form a new group, wasn't he getting together with Ginger Baker and Stevie Winwood again, was he going to join Crosby, Stills, Nash and Young, was he going to get John and George and start the new Beatles?

An air of mystery hung over the Clapton camp, as people speculated on the guitarist's plans. After all, he'd played on an awful lot of great records lately - John and Yoko's Live Peace in Toronto, with King Curtis on his Teasin' single, with George Harrison on his forthcoming album, and with Delaney and Bonnie on their album.

At the studio, Clapton and Steve Stills were obviously getting off on each other. Eric's hair was shorn off shorter than John and Yoko's, and it was as though Clapton had discarded his old hang-ups along with the hair.

He beamed at everyone. No longer moody, no longer introverted, Eric was simply having a good time. His only concern was that people would accept his singing on his new album.

He was immaculately dressed in a patchwork silk shirt, green velvet pants, black patent high-heeled boots and a magnificent brown suede vest.

And he was more than keen to talk about anything we mentioned.

Q **Let's first talk about the tracks on your new album.**

The first track on side one will be the instrumental we did, which was just a good day of recording in Los Angeles, when Leon Russell came along. It was just a jam. Sounds nice, I'm really pleased with it. It's also matched to another track on the album called Blues Power, which is a song that Leon wrote. The words are really applicable to me.

And then there's Lonesome and a Long Way from Home which is a song that Delaney Bramlett wrote a long time ago. Originally he did it acoustically, and the Hertz people were trying to buy it from him for a commercial. He was doing it with King Curtis when I arrived in LA and Curtis didn't like his voice on it. Curtis doesn't sing much but he's a great singer. So I said I'd like to do a version of it.

The next one, After Midnight, is a song that JJ Cale wrote. He's one of those people from Tulsa and I think he's an engineer now. He made a record of it and I dug the record a lot so we did our version of that.

Lovin' You, Lovin' Me started out as a song that Delaney and Leon wrote for Blind Faith to do. I liked it very much. I don't know if the others ever heard it. I said I wanted to do it if I ever did a solo album, so we changed it around a bit to suit the way I could sing it and cut it in England.

I Don't Know Why is a ballad, a love song kind of thing. It was an idea that Delaney had when he came to England, and we finished it while he was staying at my house. We recorded it once in London, and again in Los Angeles.

Get Up and Get Your Man a Bottle of Red Wine is a ballad too. We were going to the studio one day in LA and we had no songs, nothing at all to do. We were getting panicky on the way and we just thought up the song and did it when we got there. It's just a shuffle.

I've already mentioned Blues Power. It feels like he wrote it for me. I don't want to be pretentious and say he did, but it's easy to sing and it's exactly what I wanted to say.

I Told You for the Last Time is a song that Delaney played on acoustic guitar. One of his motel shot numbers I think. We changed that around and arranged it for a big band sort of feel and it came out like a country number really.

The last one is called She Rides. That just came from the lyrics of the original song we wrote. But when we went into the studio, the track came off so well that we abandoned the original song and since then I've been trying to think up a set of lyrics to go with the track. That's what has been holding the album up.

(This interview was taped before the release of the album.)

Q **It would seem that this album means a lot to you.**

A great deal. The biggest reason for it coming out for me is that it's just good music. I loved the sound of the whole thing and I never thought that was possible. I've had a great deal of hang-ups about my singing all my life. I've always been very worried about whether or not I could sing.

Q **In this case, you've certainly got the job done.**

Well, you see the thing is I got so much help that I couldn't let anybody down and I had to do it. It wasn't a question of proving anything to anybody. I just had to do it. The love that went around between everybody involved on the record was just so powerful that I'm really proud of it.

Q **There have been unsubstantiated rumours that your parting with Delaney and Bonnie in the US was not particularly friendly.**

I don't think they were based on anything very strong. The only thing that was a sort of a hassle was the fact that it was a bit hard for me to stay in America that long. I really found it very hard because I was the only one there from England except for my roadie.

It was very hard.....it was a culture shock to be alone in a place like that. I've never been alone in America before. I had always been with a group of some kind and I found I really had to stand up for myself.

It was good for me in a great many ways, but, at the time, it was very hard and sometimes I withdrew and felt that I shouldn't be there. I should be back home.

Q **How did you first get involved with Delaney and Bonnie?**

It was just a natural progression from meeting them on the Blind Faith tour - jamming with them, and hanging out with them and digging them, and really loving them as people. They helped me so much from the first moment I met them. They helped me get my thing together. Made me feel like I was someone, rather than just a musician.

Q **The help has been mutually beneficial, I would think.**

Yeah. I felt that they were getting shoved to one side by a lot of people and taken for granted just because they were American in America. It's really hard to see people in your own backyard, even if they are really good. So I thought if I brought them to England, then they could go back to the States with that as part of their reputation. And we had such a good time that I forgot about all the reasons. It was just a gas to do it, man.

Delaney and Bonnie brought a new feeling to the pop stage. With most groups, you pick up some antagonism when the act is working, but with D&B, it's all love.

It seems to me that people are too sure of themselves. So many musicians and artists just want to make a little sack of bread and then withdraw to their country estates and send out the odd albums to the

public - as though they were doing everybody a favour, and assuming that they're really on top. And it's such a change when somebody comes along who is really humble like those people are. And they're just willing to work and make very little money. They make so little because there's so many in the group all the time.

Q **This must have been a complete change for you after the trail of superstars - the Jack Bruces, the Ginger Bakers, the Stevie Winwoods.**

There is a difference. English people are different anyway. I was a great deal different until I met them. And I'm still finding it hard to get out of myself and become uninhibited. Most of the English musicians that I've played with and know are very sort of schizoid . . . they get it on when they play but when they're not playing, they're very withdrawn, sort of reticent people. That often infringes on the playing too. After a while their stuff becomes very introverted.

Q **You've always seemed to be very shy. In the Cream days, when people went up and told you that you could really play that guitar, you'd seem embarrassed by it all.**

I still am, because I think that just playing the guitar isn't enough. I really don't think it is.

Q **A lot of people would disagree with that.**

Yeah, but I just can't see it. It's very hard for me to see why someone would laud a cat who just plays the guitar. It's really not enough, somehow. If I was a great songwriter or a great singer, then I wouldn't be so humble about it. I wouldn't be shy. Until I am either a great songwriter or a great singer, then I shall carry on being embarrassed when people come on with that praise stuff.

Q How about the 'Clapton is God' buttons?

Yeah, well it's silly. It really is. It's unfounded because I haven't even started to work it out yet.

Q Did you have anything to do with the McCartney album?

No, I haven't seen or heard of Paul for years and years.

Q Is it that you like playing so much that you play with anybody, or you're trying to find what thing you dig the most?

It's both. I do enjoy playing with anybody, really just about anybody because there's always a facet of it that you can enjoy. I really don't know what I want to do most of the time, and so I often just follow the leader.

I'm an Aries you see, and there are two kinds of Aries. The two kinds are the push-forward people who shove and do whatever they want to do and step on people in the process. The other kind are the sheep, the followers. They just follow the crowd, whatever's happening. I often go between the two.

When I'm positive about what I want to do, nothing can stop me. If I've got an idea about something then nothing can change my mind. But if I'm lost for something to do then I'll follow whatever's going on. Everytime I'm doing one of those other gigs I'm probably in one of those moods. Where I just don't know so I go along to a session and just play with someone.

Q Looking back over your career, what are your recollections of John Mayall?

Well, it was like a stepping stone really. I didn't know at the time what I wanted to be, what I should do or what I should play. So I just tried to fit in with whoever I was with and the John Mayall gig - it really felt very natural for me to play with him.

Q How about Cream?

Cream I felt sort of disoriented about. Disoriented at the time I was doing it which was the trouble. It didn't coincide with the way I felt about it. The way I felt it should be. It was very strange. I still like a lot of the records we made. But there was something wrong somewhere. There was a weakness.

Q How about the rumours that Cream are getting together for another final concert tour?

I've already denied them in print but I don't suppose it's gonna make any difference to the rumours. I think it's unfair for any one of us who was involved to say I am definitely not doing it, because it's offensive to the others. I really don't think it will ever happen.

Q How about Blind Faith?

Yeah, I'd like to do some things with them, but then it's not them any more. It's either the Air Force or the Traffic. So I'll start getting together my thing. When the album comes out, I'll just sit around for a while and see if it's gonna be a popular thing. You can never be sure, it's always a gamble.

Q Is it true that you want to write religious songs?

Yeah I do. It's not just a question of wanting to. I already have written religious songs, such as In the Presence of the Lord. That's a strange song because I wrote it and then someone told me that somewhere in the scriptures it had also been written . . . the same words. I never knew that, it was an incredible coincidence.

I do find that songs of praise are one of my greatest inspirations. I constantly thank the Lord for being on the earth and for giving me the power to be able to play and entertain people. And now He's given me the power to sing and communicate, so I owe it to Him.

Q **I imagine you enjoy gospel music a lot, and people like Aretha Franklin?**

Very much. Yeah. I love it.

Q **You once did a track with Aretha - Good to Me as I am to You on the Lady Soul album.**

It was a great thrill doing it.

Q **Are you going to do any more work with Aretha?**

I'd be there if she ever wanted me to do it, you can be sure of that. That track we did was one of the best things I've ever done.

Q **I've always wondered what you thought of Led Zeppelin, which was the band that filled the vacuum created by the end of Cream and the downfall of Jimi Hendrix?**

I don't really know. I've heard their records and I saw them play in Milwaukee. . . we were doing a festival together. It was very loud, unnecessarily loud. I liked some of it, I really did like some of it. But a lot of it was just too much. They over emphasised whatever point they were making.

Q **Do you like playing festivals?**

I sometimes think it's a bit too much on a grand scale. The way I like to think of a gig is in terms of a church hall somewhere in the country. And that's really where I want to play. If I can entertain the people I live with then I think I'll really be getting somewhere.

© RITCHIE YORKE, 1970

ERIC CLAPTON *slowhand*

ERIC CLAPTON:

another crossroad

(KEITH ALTHAM, FUSION, 6 FEBRUARY 1970)

Many people think that Eric Clapton is the best guitarist in the world. A veteran of the Yardbirds, John Mayall's Bluesbreakers and Cream, all that remained for him was Blind Faith and Life magazine. Somewhere along the way Blind Faith stumbled and fell. It now lies twitching on the studio floor, although individual limbs react spasmodically: Winwood working on a solo album with ex-Traffic drummer Jim Capaldi; Grech working with George Harrison and Clapton; Ginger Baker busy being Ginger Baker. The question lingering in the mind: did Blind Faith fall or was it pushed?

Q What was the first intimation you had that Faith might not last and can you enumerate some of the reasons for its apparent collapse?

As soon as I got on the plane for America I realised that it was pretty well bound to fold soon because we were being exploited. We were doing it ourselves, in as much as we agreed to all those gigs and exposing ourselves, so we have no-one to blame but ourselves. If you get a group together, hype it and send it out on the road it will succeed to a certain extent, but it has capitulated - you don't expect a group like that to last long. If a group really wants to get together to play for a long time they have to be left alone to do it and they have to ensure they are left alone. With Blind Faith we knew we were going to make a lot of bread and that could have become the reason for its existence – it probably did become the reason and the group became secondary.

Q Was Blind Faith ever intended as a long-term proposition?

There was really no planning behind the group's formation at all. It was simply an idea that Stevie and I had to form a band - it was a miracle to me that we ever got it together to make an album. Originally, I thought that Stevie and I would make a powerful front in which Ginger could settle back behind us but, unfortunately, Stevie is a reticent musician, as I am myself in many ways, and when he hears someone trying to come through he just steps aside. The whole band was much too polite with everyone, waiting for each other to take the initiative. The group existed just as long as the individual members wanted it to be.

Q Are you saying that it is because of individual apathy that the group is dying - if so why do you not choose to get them together again yourself?

The simple truth is that since we returned from America no-one has bothered to contact me and I don't really feel that I can take it upon myself to play leader of the group - I'm not. If someone gets on the phone, like, for example, they did recently to invite me to play on the Plastic Ono Cold Turkey single, then I just go along with my guitar. If someone rang me tomorrow and said you're in the studio with Faith tomorrow I'd probably go along. But the situation is now that everyone is doing their own thing - I'm involved with Delaney and Bonnie until the New Year and so if anything is to be done, it won't be for some time.

Q Are you personally upset or disappointed by the lack of communication from the other members?

Yes I am a little but that's my own fault if anything. If I had wanted more respect from Stevie I could have gone about doing things which would have earned it - instead of which I withdrew and just played lead guitar. I mean if I had written a few more songs or written songs with him, tried more, he might have respected me more. What happened was that we both went into our shells. Stevie is a very natural guy and he shies away from anything which could be regarded as musical 'professionalism' – he doesn't like people who set out to prove themselves as musical professionals. Most of all he likes people who play lots of instruments without being particularly brilliant on anything - he likes 'unskilled musical labour', to use one of his own terms. That is something which everybody can understand that has quite a low common denominator - something that people can join in and play along rather than anything which might appear to have a high artistic level.

Q The reports of Faith's first American tour were ecstatic in the British press but were those first live appearances as satisfactory as you had hoped?

Madison Square Garden was the first gig and the reaction really excited us but it wasn't until later that I realised it was purely a political thing - there were the cops, the audience and us and it wouldn't have mattered if we had gone on and played Knees Up Mother Brown, they would still have flipped out. We played a few places that were half-empty but that was

slowhand **ERIC CLAPTON** | **15**

our own fault too because we deliberately played down the use of our own names. People heard on the radio that 'Blind Faith' were in town and thought 'who's Blind Faith for crying out loud - never heard of them'. We had specifically said not to use our names but if we had there would probably have been a lot more people who would have come to see Winwood, Baker or Clapton.

There were really three different phases with Blind Faith. It was a totally different concept when just Steve and I were getting it together down at his cottage in Berkshire with our friends, and to my way of thinking that was probably the best phase which produced the best results because we were just playing for ourselves we were not trying to prove anything or achieve anything - just playing to have a good time. But when we got together with Rick and Ginger in the studios for the album it changed there completely, and when we went on stage it changed again.

Q **Several critics seemed to think that Faith were missing the kind of guiding hand on the production of the album that there was with Cream. What do you think?**

That could be true but it should be understood that Jimmy Miller was called in at very late notice half way through the album because we had such an incredible deadline to meet and we only had a third of the album finished. Jimmy had the unenviable job of cleaning up after us and getting together what we had already cut and then trying to find out what we were trying to achieve. I think he was really confused through most of the sessions because nobody seemed to know what we were doing, everyone was guessing and improvising on the spot. We should have had someone to say 'what we are doing is country rock and roll with a bit of electric church on the side', but no-one did and we just told him to sit down and produce it.

Q **One critic in Life magazine wrote that Faith were comprised of three rock 'n' roll stars and one rock 'n' roll clod – Rick Grech. What's your reaction to that?**

Oh, my God, what a fucking pathetic thing to say! I've had people say that kind of thing about me. What can I say? Rick plays versatile country violin, good classical violin, and can adapt to a rock 'n' roll idiom and still make it sound palatable. He plays 'cello, and electric bass and if that is the work of a 'clod' you can bracket me with him. I take very little notice of what the majority of critics say because even the most informed usually put their foot in it and show themselves up for complete naivety when it comes to music. I heard one self-styled critic on the radio recently playing The Band's Cripple Creek. After he had played it he said, 'Oh well, I don't know who that is and I'm sure you don't and it's a bore anyway so we won't bother to buy it, will we?' That's all you need to know about him - from there on in you disregard most everything he says. Most critics are competitive-minded and they can't say something good without comparing to something else - they're always saying let's take the Blind Faith album and compare it with Humble Pie and say one is good and the other is not - it's not necessary and it's hopelessly inadequate.

Q In view of the 'comparative' failure of Blind Faith to motor on, do you have any regrets in retrospect about leaving so successful a unit as Cream?

Cream were a source of great confusion to me - it had to end and I don't think I could be a part of something like that now. Musically its significance was rather like Pete Townshend said - 'a product of that time' - symbolic of en era. It became a very heavy virtuoso thing without anyone really contributing to a whole. I don't think there will ever be another group to take its place for success, you know, unless it invents a new formula because we were the first trio and the first kind of virtuoso people to do it. The strange thing about Cream was that every time we went into the studios to record we formed another group, adding violins or another guitar or something. The virtuoso thing was a substitute for the fact that I wasn't singing myself, that I wasn't expressing myself through my words and my music and so I had to force it through a guitar. It's the same now - except I have the guitar better controlled. But I feel the same frustrations.

Q Why have you never made the attempt to form your own group and write more of your own material if you feel the limitations of working within the confines of other groups?

I need someone to give me a good kick up the arse to get me going. I'm a lazy sort of person and I need incentive. I keep thinking, well, next week I'll sit down

and write ten songs and that keeps me going because I don't have to worry about making money any more - I can live off what I have earned. I suppose I am a musical drifter to most people but I have always intended to do my own thing eventually - it's just that every time I get around to it something else crops up. My life is really my work - I don't think I can do anything of which I would be a 100 per cent proud but it keeps me going. As a guitarist I am seeking refinement, that is the simplest and most effective way of saying the thing exactly as you want to. But as an individual I am seeing self-expression on more totalitarian lines, I would like to be able to make my own albums and be able to promote them myself - go on television and do shows myself with my own group - that's my goal, if you like.

Q It would appear that possibly your closest friend within the business is George Harrison. Can you explain what it is that has promoted that association?

It's a question of mutual respect. I have a great deal of respect for him because there have probably been a thousand times when he wanted to quit the Beatles and do something on his own, but he never has. In fact, he is probably the one in the Beatles who has done most of the patching up - he is their mediator and his philosophical outlook has been one of the primary reasons that has kept them together. Paradoxically, he respects me for having the courage to walk out on groups because I don't like what I am doing. He has often said to me that he does not see me in any band for very long and I think he has a strange regard for my facing up to impossible situations and just cutting out. I try to put my restlessness behind me when I get involved in a new group but it always seems to reappear and defeat me in the end.

Q **Having worked with Lennon on the Plastic Ono Band what kind of an association do you have with him?**

I have certain ideas in sympathy with him but he has the single-mindedness which can help him say things he believes and put those convictions in his work. I admire that but I avoid that kind of responsibility because I don't really think it is necessary for any musician to be a leader of the people - if you are going to do it, then his way is probably the best.

Q **On the last occasion I saw you, we were at the Dylan Isle of Wight Festival - what was your reaction to Dylan '69?**

I don't think he's stepped back and he seems very conscious of his own influence still - people have lived their lives by his songs and his latest songs still govern attitudes. People seemed to think that Nashville Skyline was some kind of cop-out but he was still giving good advice - you couldn't give better advice or more simple advice than 'Throw it all away'.

Q **Would you like to restate your position over the question of drugs and their use - it seems as though a number of influential musicians, namely Donovan and Townshend, have come out of the drug thing at the other end actively opposed to any form of drugs - including alcohol in Townshend's case.**

I haven't actually had anything which has told me otherwise. I'm not going to believe what someone else says about it and if someone says don't take 'em I'm not going to simply take their word for it. If I took something which reacted adversely or unpleasantly upon me I would stop taking it. It is a very escapist thing and something which I personally would not indulge in during time when I need to concentrate heavily. But when I've got nothing to do then it's a strong temptation and one which I do not resist. Pot to most people is a kind of crutch but what really requires stronger definition is the word 'addiction' and the word 'habit-forming' - I mean I'm addicted to this rocking chair I'm in. People escape with pot and who says that they have no right to do so - because someone points out that life really is beautiful is not going to stop some poor soul rotting in a cellar, waving his hands in disgust and rolling a joint. People should be instilled with hope - it's a thing you can't live without but there's no guarantee that you will get anything from hoping! The dangers of over-using, misusing or abusing drugs should be obvious simply by looking at those people who get themselves in the state where they think it all happens in your head and ends there, whereas, in fact, the manifestation of all those fantasies are the important things and pot is often obstructing that. It's what you share with people that matters. I try to share my music with people.

the rolling stone interview:
ERIC CLAPTON

(STEVE TURNER, ROLLING STONE, 18 JULY 1974)

London - Robert Stigwood, his manager, put it about as simply and as playfully as it could be put, after a celebration party in April: 'Old Slowhand is back'. Eric Clapton, who had been called everything from good to God during a roller-coaster ride as one of rock's leading guitar players of the 60s, was emerging from the mire of three years of silence punctuated only by two benefit concert appearances and rumours of heroin addiction. Now, with a new album, 461 Ocean Boulevard due for release this month, and a 23-date US tour under way, Clapton has returned.

'Slowhand' was the ironic nickname for Clapton, who is 29, when his style - fluid, creative blues phrases - came to general attention in 1964 with the Yardbirds. Rock criticism crackled with the notion that a pioneer stylist had been spawned, and waited, often in awe, for him to fulfill the potential.

He left the Yardbirds in 1965, spurning the group's turn from blues to commercial rock, and put in two years as lead guitar with John Mayall's Bluebreakers, a period that saw him and his audience hewing a tight line as 'blues purists'. By 1967, though, the form, as expressed by the Bluebreakers, had become too rigid, and he left to form, with Ginger Baker and Jack Bruce, the seminal power trio, Cream.

The group exploded with such force - sheer loudness and solo extrapolation within a theme being its innovations - that some saw it (as some still do) as the be-all and end-all of rock. The group disbanded in 1969, after four gold albums and a triumphant 'goodbye' tour - again because Clapton sensed his playing becoming clichéd. Clapton fanatics waited in salivation for his next move.

What followed, though, was Blind Faith (Clapton, Baker, Rick Grech and Steve Winwood) - a supergroup adventure that quickly was written off by both the performers and the audience as a media hype.

Clapton came right back, touring and recording with Delaney and Bonnie Bramlett in 1970, using the same loose group of 'friends' for an Eric Clapton album, and picking three of them - Carl Radle, Bobby Whitlock and Bobby Keys - for Derek and the Dominos.

Along with Duane Allman, they cut an album in Miami in 1970, then, without Allman, toured in 1971. Like Cream, Derek and the Dominos convinced a sizeable audience - both critical and popular - that it finally had heard what music was all about.

Throughout the high-energy thrust of those years, Clapton was acclaimed in quarters large and small. Melody Maker's 'World's Top Musician' in 1969. Guitar Player's 'Best Guitar Player in the World' in 1970. He was known as 'King of the Blues Guitarists', and the New Musical Express said of his work with Cream, 'the kind of guitar playing upon which legends are built.' The topper, though, appeared in a subway station in 1965, and spread over the walls of London: 'Clapton is God'.

Behind the sensations and the obvious success, Clapton was a shy ('painfully', some said) and humble (so said many reporters) personality. He confined his excesses - minor league destructo pranks like pouring Pete Townshend into an egg-and-flour pudding concocted in a shower stall - to friends and other musicians. He was, outside his music, pretty much anonymous.

Then, following the Derek and the Dominos tour, he disappeared, playing only at the Concert for Bangladesh in 1971 and the Rainbow Concert in London in 1973. His absence spawned rumours - that he was an addict, that he was dying, that he was dead - and, in the necro-gossipy atmosphere following the deaths of Janis Joplin and Jimi Hendrix, he was one of rock's stars accorded the bizarre title, 'most likely to die next'.

For a three-year period Clapton was silent, playing no new music outside his home, granting no interviews, ducking reporters. Now, comfortable enough that he brought up the subject of addiction himself, he has emerged. We met through a mutual friend, near the end of February.

The interview was conducted in four sessions, the first three of which took place while he was undergoing electro-acupuncture treatment (a method developed in China and only recently introduced in the West) for heroin addiction. He was despondent at first, speaking of 'the waste of the last three years' and saying he couldn't see a glimmer of hope for the future. 'I still feel that to be a junkie is to be a part of a very elite club', he said. 'I've also got this death wish. I don't like life. That's another reason for taking heroin, because it's like surrounding yourself in pink cotton wool. Nothing bothers you whatsoever, man. Nothing will phase you out in any way.'

The treatment completed, Clapton went to Wales, where he worked on a farm for a short time. He then returned to his country home in Surrey, and within three weeks had made the decision to record and tour. On 10th April, Stigwood threw the celebration party for him in London, and a few days later Clapton was off to Miami to record 461 Ocean Boulevard.

The final interview took place in Surrey, after his return to England in May. He was relaxed and confident, eager to get on with the tour, pleased with the album, and downright disinterested in dope.

Q **Why the three-year layoff?**

I'd overexposed myself. I'd worked so hard and played in front of so many people that it frightened me into hiding for a bit. And I think it's probably going to happen again. I'll go out and work, and play for three years and then for the next three years I'll go and hibernate somewhere else! You can't keep at it all the time, I'm sure of that.

Q **So how've you been spending your time?**

Hibernating! I played a lot. I played here at home probably more than I do now but without really getting anything done. Just keeping my hand in.

Q **Were you writing at all?**

Sometimes, but most of the stuff I did in that period was so gloomy that I wouldn't use it now. Also, when you sit and play on your own you write on an acoustic guitar and so if you try and place it in the context of a band it doesn't mean a thing. You have to get back out...

Q **...to the road?**

Oh, yeh. I've been sitting around here for a week now and I'm getting really edgy, bored. Because for those three weeks in Miami it just cooked so fast and so strong we should have perhaps gone straight to a gig from there instead of taking a pause. But I'm sure we'll pick up the threads.

Q **Were you surprised to get things going so quickly in Miami?**

Yeh, yeh. I was very worried when I got there. I had the panics. It took me a couple of days just to learn to create from nothing - to groove on whatever was happening, and then it was all right. But I always get that when I sit down and think about something. I've got it now about the tour to a certain extent. Whether or not we can get all the people to come and see us, that kind of thing, which is so silly, really. It's only when you sit down and worry about it that you ever think about it at all.

Q **You say you always needed pain to create and yet you enjoyed heroin because it took away the pain. How do you explain that one?**

I mean, I enjoy the pain in a way because I know I

can make use of it if I don't tamper with it. You can take away the pain in a way by playing the guitar, just making music and seeing people enjoying themselves on it. The thing that knocked me out most of all about getting off was the fact that I could feel again, you know. I don't care where I'm going, up or down, or whatever they do to me, as long as they let me keep my feelings.

Q **Did you feel they'd been excluded?**

Yeh, well, I'd done that to myself, you see. Because at the time we were doing Layla, my feelings were so intense that I just couldn't handle it. So that's why I started to cancel them out and that in turn becomes the pain. People used to come around here and try and shake me off by the scruff of the neck and say come on, get out, come with me. I mean, people even considered kidnapping me and taking me somewhere where I'd have to get myself together. And like that's the pain, the fact that afterwards you realise all the people you hurt by doing that.

Q **So it was the crisis that happened around 'Layla' time that sent you into it?**

Yeah. There were quite a lot of factors involved. Also, I mean, I used to go on about how I wanted to have a voice like Ray Charles and everyone had said that he was one of those, that he had that problem, and that's why he sang like that. Now I know that that is utter bullshit. I've got the first album that he made and his voice there was unbelievable, you know, and it's just got nothing to do with what you take or what you put

Pictorial Press

in your bloodstream.

Q Whose music turns you on now?

Whenever I put my new album on and start to think it sounds great, I always put Stevie Wonder on afterwards just to get my pulse down again! He's the one for me. I think he's got it well covered. I think when it comes down to it, I always go for singers. I don't buy an album because I like the lead guitar. I always like the human voice most of all.

Q What's your domestic background?

I was semi-adopted. I was brought up by my grandparents because my mother went away when I was very young and got married to someone. So I've got a stepfather but I don't see them because they've got a family themselves and they live in Canada. From there I just grew up in all the local schools around Ripley in Surrey and went to art school (Kingston Art College).

Q What sort of kid were you at school?

I was the one that used to get stones thrown at me because I was so thin and couldn't do physical training very well! One of those types. I was always the seven-stone (98-pound) weakling. I used to hang out with three or four other kids who were all in that same kind of predicament. The outcasts. They used to call us the loonies.

Q What effect did that have on you?

It was quite nice in a way because we started up a little clique. Although we were underprivileged, we were the first ones to get Buddy Holly records and things like that. I mean, we were considered freaks because of things like that.

Q What happened at art school?

I played records in the lunch break most of the time! That's also where I started to play guitar and began listening to blues records all the time.

Q Who in particular?

Muddy Waters, Big Bill Broonzy... I could go on for hours. There's no point. Just the blues.

Q How did you get to hear these records in the first place?

I think they used to play a couple of them on the radio. It's unbelievable that things like that were getting through but they were. Chuck Berry was getting played and I definitely heard Big Bill Broonzy records on the radio. And Sonny Terry and Brownie McGhee. I used to get catches of these things which sounded much better than Jimmy Young, Max Bygraves and Frankie Vaughan to me. So I started looking around and buying them. I still started out by liking Holly and Berry and people like that who were the first things I ever bought, but then I'd read things on the back of album covers like, 'rock 'n' roll has its roots in blues', and stuff like that. And so I thought, what's that all about? I'll have to find out.

Q How were you performing at this point?

Casually, I wasn't professional, didn't have a band. I was just a blues aficionado with a guitar attempting to sing. When Mick (Jagger) got a sore throat I used to get up and dep. for him at the Ealing club.

Q Were the old days 'good' old days?

Of course. Yeah, lovely times. Probably because it was another clique thing. We felt honored to be members of this sort of club of people who just liked rhythm and blues records. It was like security in a way, and it was nice... I feel much more alone these days. Whatever I've got to achieve, I've got to achieve on my own. In the old days it seemed that there was always a crowd you hung out with.

Q **What happened after that?**

I bummed around for a bit. I tried busking around Kingston and Richmond and, of course, it was the beat scene then so if you sat in a pub and played San Franscisco Bay Blues and stuff like that, you'd get a drink and a sandwich and perhaps even somewhere to sleep for the night. Then my mum and dad, that's to say my grandparents, were getting a bit pissed off because I obviously wasn't making a name for myself in their eyes, so I went to work with my old man on the building site for a couple of months. And that was good fun. At the same time, I was playing clubs in the evenings with a band called the Roosters. Brian Jones and Paul Jones were in the band before me but they'd both gone their separate ways - Paul with Manfred Mann and Brian with the Stones.

Q **Did Casey Jones and the Engineers come next?**

Oh, dear! Yeah. Didn't last long though. But it got my chops together. It was all good experience. The Mersey thing was just happening and to be in a group like Casey Jones and the Engineers, I mean, you got a few good gigs just because he was a Liverpudlian.

Q **Were you an original member of the Yardbirds?**

No. They'd already been going a couple of months and they'd had a lead guitarist who'd quit, or they'd chucked him out, and just by word of mouth I got the job. Then they wanted to make a hit record and I wasn't ready for that at that time. I probably never have been unless it's on my terms. But they thought that if they changed what they wore and did more Top 40-type material they would get a hit record, and that's just exactly when I left them. I played on the record (For Your Love / Got to Hurry), it was OK, but I could see it was a pop tune written for the purpose of getting into the charts and nothing else. I think I left after the session. I was only out of work for a couple of weeks, though, and then John Mayall called me up and said, would I like to be in his band, and that suited me fine because it was a blues band and I was going through my purist number then. So it suited me down to the ground. For me, in those days, blues was the only kind of music and I didn't like anything else.

Q **When you left Mayall to form Cream, were you at all influenced by Jimi Hendrix's Experience?**

No. We'd been going about two weeks when he came to England. I remember Chas (Chandler) brought him to one of our gigs. We were playing somewhere in London and we jammed and I thought, my god! I couldn't believe it! It really blew my mind. Totally. And then he got a three-piece together.

Q **How did all this affect your music?**

It opened it up a lot because I was still at that time

pretty uptight by the fact that we weren't playing 100 per cent blues numbers, and to see Jimi play that way I just thought, Wow! That's all right with me! It just sort of opened my mind up to listening to a lot of other things and playing a lot of other things. Jimi and I always had a friendship from a distance because we never really spent a lot of time together - only during the acid period I used to see him a lot. Occasionally we'd spend time alone together just raving about, but, I mean, it was always a distant friendship. Playing together was something else.

Q How early on in Cream's existence were you dissastisfied?

After the Fillmore (1967) we did a tour that went on for five months - one-nighters. That did me in completely. I just experimented one night - I stopped playing halfway through a number and the other two didn't notice, you know! I just stood there and watched and they carried on playing 'till the end of the number. I thought, well, fuck that, you know! You see, Cream was originally meant to be a blues trio, like Buddy Guy with a rhythm section. I wanted to be Buddy Guy, the guitarist with a good rhythm section.

Q What sort of gigs did you intend to play?

Small clubs. We didn't want to be big in any way.

Q When did you realise things weren't turning out this way?

The Windsor Jazz and Blues Festival 1966, which was almost our first gig. We found that we ran out of numbers so quickly that we just had to improvise.

Pictorial Press

So we just made up 12-bar blues and that became Cream. That became what we were known for. I liked it up to a point, but it wasn't what I wanted.

Q Why did you release Wrapping Paper as your first single when it was so un-Cream and unblues?

Well, another idea we had with Cream was to be totally dada and have weird things onstage and stuff like that. It never really happened but Wrapping Paper, I suppose, was part of that kind of attitude. You know - put out something weird! We did one gig at the Marquee where we had a gorilla onstage and stuff like that - dry ice, freaky things. No meaning, no purpose... just lunacy!

Q Do you think press reaction affected Cream in the end?

Do you really want me to bring that up? You see, there was a constant battle between Jack and Ginger because they loved one another's playing but couldn't stand one another's sight. I was the mediator and I was getting tired of that and then this Rolling Stone (No. 10, 11th May 1968) came out with an interview with me boosting my ego followed on the next page by a concert review deflating it, calling me 'the master of the cliché', which knocked me cold. At that point in time I decided that I was leaving Cream. Also, another interesting factor was that I got the tapes of Music from Big Pink and I thought, well, this is what I want to play - not extended solos and maestro bullshit but just good funky songs. The combination of that Rolling Stones thing and hearing Big Pink decided for me that I was going to split Cream.

Q What about the fact that, as you've already told me, the audiences were responding to music which you weren't happy with. Where does that come in?

Well, once we'd got our wings we couldn't play a note wrong. I thought, this isn't right because the music we're playing is useless. OK, it has its moments but it's not what they deserve. They're paying too much, they're applauding too much and it makes me feel like a con man. I don't want to feel like a con man. I want to feel that I've earned what I've got. You see, it got to the point where we were playing so badly and the audience was still going raving mad - they thought it was a gas. But I thought, we're cheating them. We're taking their bread and playing them shit. I can't work on that basis.

Q You said that you'd never been happy with your performance with Cream, although you'd got a couple of good licks in here and there.

With Cream we had our ups and downs. We had good gigs and bad gigs. We had gigs when you could have mistaken us for Hendrix, it was that good, and other times we were like the worst band in the world. It was this kind of inconsistency that relied upon the improvisation factor. All our songs had a starting theme, a finishing theme, and a middle that was up to us. On a good night it was great and on a bad night it was awful. I couldn't take this kind of up and down. So I got in a few good licks while Cream was going. But like on Farewell we did Badge and I liked that.

It was all because I played them Big Pink and said, 'look, this is what music is all about, let's try and get a sound like this' - that we got the sound like Badge and the rest. After I left Cream, let's see... what did I do? It was Blind Faith wasn't it? Almost straight away? Well, I promised Ginger that whatever I did, I'd take him with me because we had a close thing going. So, what happened was that we didn't rehearse enough, we didn't get to know each other enough, we didn't go through enough trials and tribulations before the big time came. We went straight into the big gigs and I came offstage shaking like a leaf because I felt once again that I'd let people down. There are 36,000 people waiting there for what you're going to do and if it's not what you think is right - no way! And then I met Delaney and Bonnie on the second night of the '67 American tour and they were just such down home humble cats and they were getting very little applause, very little money, and the only reason they were on the bill was because I'd asked for them to be the second act. So I started a rapport with Delaney, which became very strong and severed my relationship with Blind Faith. So, Blind Faith was breaking up in that Stevie and Ginger were arguing. Rick was kind of in the middle and I was out altogether. I was with Delaney and Bonnie. I already saw ahead that I didn't want Blind Faith. I wanted to be lead guitarist with Delaney and Bonnie because they were singing soul music.

Q **Initially, what did you think you could have done with Blind Faith that you couldn't have done with Cream?**

I didn't know. I never have that positive an idea of what direction I'm going in. I mean, I just thought, Cream's got to go, but I still want to play, and I'd always wanted to play with Stevie because I knew that he was a very laid-back musician.

Q **So, ultimately, why didn't it work out?**

Because we rehearsed for three weeks, publicised and all that hype, and the first audience we played to was 36,000 people at Hyde Park, London!

Q **Why did you allow this to happen?**

We had no control over it. We just sort of went along, we thought it would be all right. All the time we were touring, though. I was hanging out with Delaney and Bonnie because they were getting no money, bottom of the bill and no-one was clapping them, and we were being adulated and all that rubbish and getting lots of bread. I think I did the right thing going off with them and then stealing the Dominos away from them, you know. But the funny thing was that once I'd got Layla out of my system, I didn't want to do any more with the Dominos. I didn't want to play another note.

Q **How did you get into singing?**

It was something Delaney said and it was also something Lord Buckley said, which is that if God gives you a talent and you don't use it, then He'll take it away. If you don't put it to use you won't be able to use it when you want to use it.

Q **How did you feel about the Rainbow gig?**

I thought it was OK. I had a good time doing it. It was

when I listened to the tapes afterwards that I realised that it was well under par.

Q **What specific musical criticism did you have?**

It's hard to remember now. I think the music was reasonably OK, I just think that there were too many people onstage for the way it was recorded. They recorded it on something like an eight-track and so they had to mix a lot of things together while they were recording it, which meant that the rhythm section suffered and you get the bass and drums mixed in together.

Q **So you weren't disappointed with your licks?**

Well, I mean, I didn't think they were great. They were reasonable. Everyone made mistakes and what I heard when I heard the tapes back was how many mistakes we all made. But then I'm very self-critical in that way.

Q **Was Bangladesh a similar situation?**

That was quite a lot different and I just had to do it again. Because of George, you know. If he asks me to do anything, he's got the best that I can give whenever I can give it. I did it, but again I thought, no way. I mean, I was laid up sick for a week while all the rehearsals were going on, you see. Everyone got there a week early for the gig and I got very ill and couldn't move. I was literally in a very bad way. So I missed all the rehearsals, I just got there in time for the first show. So, I mean, just being in tune was enough of a problem for me. I really felt they were carrying my weight, in a way.

Q **Is there any particular song of yours which you**

prize over all the rest?

Yeh, but that's only because it's one of the last I put on record. It's on the new album. I'm proud of two of them. One's called Gimme Strength and one's called Let it Grow. Yeah, I am proud of them because they were done very quickly and they sound good on record and they were the last things I achieved. I'm never going to be that proud of stuff I've done in the past. Before this album the only thing that meant anything to me was Layla, which was because it was actually about an emotional experience, a woman that I felt really deeply about and who turned me down, and I had to kind of pour it out in some way. So we wrote these songs, made an album, and the whole thing was great.

Q **What did the woman in question think?**

She didn't give a damn.

Q **Did you ever think you could say things to her through the album that maybe you couldn't face to face? Did you ever think you'd get through to her that way?**

Yeah, yeah. Yeah, I did think that. And also the emotional content of some of the blues on it, you know. But no, man. I mean, her husband is a great musician. It's the wife-of-my-best-friend scene and her husband has been writing great songs for years about her and she still left him. You see, he grabbed one of my chicks and so I thought I'd get even with him one day, on a petty level, and it grew from that, you know. She was trying to attract his attention, trying to make him jealous, and so she used me, you see, and I fell madly in love with

her. If you listen to the words of Layla: 'I tried to give you consolation/When your old man had let you down/Like a fool, I fell in love with you/You turned my whole world upside down'.

Q **Did you need to go through a crisis to write?**

Yeh, I think I did.

Q **Where did the name Layla come from?**

It comes from a Persian love story written in the eleventh or twelvelth century, a sort of love story, that's all. It's called Layla And Majnun.

Q **Did Layla reject Majnun then?**

No, neither of them rejects the other. It's like boy meets girl but parents don't dig it.

Q **That was nothing to do with your experience, was it?**

Not really. It was just that I liked the name and the story was beautifully written. I related to it in that way.

Q **Did you consciously write Layla as a concept album about unrequited love?**

Well, it was the heaviest thing going on at the time so, yeh, I suppose it came about like that. I didn't consciously do it, though, it just happened that way. That was what I wanted to write about most of all.

Q **I heard that you had a spiritual revelation when you were in the States before this?**

Two guys came to my dressing room. They were just two Christians and they said, 'can we pray with you?' I mean, what can you do? So we knelt down and prayed and it was really like the blinding light and I said: "What's happening? I feel much better!" And then I said to them: "Let me show you this poster I've got of Jimi Hendrix." I pulled it out and there was a portrait of Christ inside which I hadn't bought, had never seen in my life before. And it just knocked the three of us sideways. From then on I became a devout Christian until this situation occurred - the three... the triangle.

Q How did that knock you out?

It just knocked me out that... he'd been into Transcendental Meditation for so long and yet couldn't keep his wife... I mean, his wife just didn't want to know. All she wanted was for him to say, 'I love you', and all he was doing was meditating. That shook my faith completely. I still pray and I still see God in other people more than I see Him in the sky or anything like that.

Q In 1970 you were quoted as saying you now wanted to write songs about Jesus.

That was probably when I moved down here. That's when I wrote Presence of the Lord. You see, I was on the run, for a start. Pilcher (a well-known London policeman) was after me. He wanted me because he was a groupie cop. He got George and he got John and Mick and the rest of them. So I was on the run from flat to flat and when I finally got out of town the pressure was off. It was such a relief, man, and it was just such a beautiful place that I sat down and wrote the song.

Q So you were superimposing your religious experience onto the actual situation of being on the run? Rather like the early Negro spirituals?

Exactly. At the time you couldn't separate the two things. It was the first song I ever wrote.

Q How do you feel about 'Cream vacuum' bands such as Mountain and Grand Funk?

I think it's OK. I think that's great, you know. I mean, I'm honoured, in a way, that they felt like doing it that way. We must have done something good in order for them to want to carry it on. It relates in a way to people going around saying, 'Isn't it a drag that Jimi's dead. There'll never be another guitarist like him'. I turned on the radio in the car the other day and I thought, that's weird, that's Jimi and I've never heard that track before, and it turned out to be a guy called Robin Trower who used to play for Procol Harum. I mean, it's great. In a way Jimi's still alive because as long as you don't forget, you preserve. I must admit, though, that I've never gone out of my way to listen to any of them. I'm very segregational like that. There are very few white bands whose records I'd actually buy. I like to listen to black music anyway. If I'd have been introduced to their music by someone, if someone had played it to me and said, 'Look, this is nice', I'd listen to it. But if I walk into a record shop I know I always go for the blues rack or the soul rack, you know, not the heavy metal rack at all.

Q How did you feel about being voted one of the rock world's next fatalities?

I thought, great, you know! They're never going to get me. I don't care what they say. I mean, they like to create that kind of mystique, I know. They want to get a lot of people there to see if so-and-so's going to die onstage. I mean, think what an event that'd be! But it's all a joke. I'm sure they don't really mean it. You see, Keith (Richards) was top of the list and what would they do if Keith died? They'd feel pretty sorry about putting that in their paper for a start... It's vicarious... they want to see someone else do it, see if they can get their rocks off that way. Well, I'm a bit like that myself - not to the extent that I'd want to see someone die onstage - but I remember I used to go to Ronnie Scott's club when the house drummer would literally come out of the dressing room and crawl across the floor because that's the only kind of energy he had. And then he'd get behind the kit and it was magic! I'm impressed by that kind of thing, very definitely.

Q **How is your relationship with Robert Stigwood?** Sort of, er, humorous! If I take him too seriously, then I start to have doubts about it all. I think he's a good businessman and he's definitely very fond of making money and the thing is he'll look after you. I mean, he looked after me when I wasn't making money. I was definitely not living up to my part of the contract and yet he never actually came down on me very heavy about it at all. He just waited for me to make up my mind that I was going to play again and then he gets on the ball, calls up promoters.

Q **Again, why do you think people will be surprised at the new album?** Because I'm still being thought of as the lead guitarist

Pictorial Press

and that's not me, it really isn't. I'm just an unskilled labourer musician who finds it difficult to get in tune, let alone play the lead guitar solos. What I tried to achieve on that album was satisfying the people I was playing with. That's what I really like doing - just sitting down with people who play anything and finding the lowest common denominator that we can all groove with and getting something going. It's not - who's going to take the front now? I mean, you take the front now, I'll take the front now! It's everyone together, all at the same time.

Q So what's your function in the new band?

The leader of the band. Occasionally I'll hit a lick that'll blow someone's mind, I know that. And if it's not mine, it'll be someone else's, only they can't have it all the time. That's probably what people want - just one long lead guitar solo.

Q To your mind, is the album related to blues?

Well, it's a funny kind of album in that way because it's got several different kinds of things on it, because I'm always worrying about who I'm going to please apart from pleasing myself. So there's probably, like, a couple of blues things on there and a couple of slightly folky things and a bit of rock as well.

Q Does the fact that you're playing less intense music mark a change in attitude?

It's not a change in attitude so much as a ...change in attitude! It's loitering with intense! No, really I'd like it to be that way, but I know that when I get up onstage I'm going to be very tempted to play loud and get

nasty and do lots of naughty things with my guitar, but I'm fighting it with everything I've got. It does you in, all that, it really does. I'll tell you about something. Once with the Dominos we dropped some acid in San Francisco, of all places to drop acid, and apart from the fact that the guitar was made of rubber, every bad lick I had, every naughty lick, blues lick... whatever you want to call it, turned the audience into all these devils in sort of red coats and things. And then I'd play a sweet one and they all turned into angels. I prefer playing to angels, personally.

Q A good enough reason!

It is, when you think about it. It is, I mean, I just hate to think what all that heavy music is doing to all these poor people in terms of ...like, eating raw meat. It's the same kind of thing, do you know what I mean? The seeds that you sow are the ones that you reap. If you're going to make everyone feel naughty, then they'll be naughty and we can't have that.

Q What about the George Harrison tour rumours which sounded good to your ears when you first heard them?

They still do sound good except that he's got a lot on his plate at the moment, let alone thinking about touring. Sure, I'd love to work with him onstage. I really would. But he's got his own fish to fry and so've I.

Q What's the best Eric Clapton rumor that you've heard?

That there are strong chances that I'll be committed very soon! Actually, I've heard some funny rumours about me, you know, about what I'm supposed to be doing, where I am, what I have been doing... and none of them were anywhere near it, really.

Q Perhaps that's what comes of not giving interviews!

No, it doesn't really. They'll still... 'cos I'll still hedge even with my mates, let alone what I say to the press. I mean, it's rumours. I even tell rumours about myself. It's all speculation.

Q You've been acting in Ken Russell's film of Tommy?

Oh, yes. Phew, that was quite a number, I can tell you! Acting out a part! They had this church hall... I mean, it wasn't mucking about. They had me there to play the preacher and I had to be the preacher 'cos they had about 60 or 70 people who really were in a bad way. Well, I mean, they say they're in a bad way. They couldn't keep their arms under control, couldn't see and all that, and it was quite heavy having to be their preacher for the day. Tommy's looking for a cure and I'm just one of the geezers he goes to and it doesn't work again. He still can't see and hear. The thing about it is that it's about this chick who can heal you if you kiss her feet. I mean, she's not there - it's a statue of her, and the chick is Marilyn Monroe. So they've got this big statue of Marilyn Monroe and they're leading all these blind people and paraplegics and kissing her feet and I'm the loony in charge.

Q Do you have to play guitar?

Yeh. Well, I had it around my neck. I have to sing The

Hawker - Richie Havens did it on the Tommy album.

Q Do you ever think beyond the end of this tour?

I can't even face tomorrow. It's going to be another three years before they wear me out. And apparently, because of my tax problems, I've got to do one of those Stones numbers - you know, I've got to leave the country for a year at some point because they've, well, got me by the short and curlies, I can tell you. So, I'm on the move. I'm on the road. It don't matter. They'll never get me. They can take my body but they can't have anything else!

© STEVE TURNER, 1974

40 | **ERIC CLAPTON** slowhand

ERIC CLAPTON:
farther on up the road

(BARBARA CHARONE, SOUNDS, 9 OCTOBER 1976)

Drought? What drought? The green green grass of Surrey looks so healthy you'd think the local farmers had been secretly pumping chlorophyl injections into the earth all summer long. So much for aesthetic beauty. There was trouble. We were late. Five days late. Already I'd missed the once in a lifetime opportunity of witnessing the Cranleigh Ploughing Match. Driving past the site of this annual event, well kept fields supplied fertile proof that the competition had been fierce. So much for agricultural gamesmanship.

The roads become increasingly narrow as the car wends it's way towards Hurtwood Edge, a suitably sensitive name for the sprawling country retreat Eric Clapton calls home. Past the local and down the long and winding road, an idyllic atmosphere comfortably permeates the fresh air. So much for the introduction.

Just after two on a pleasant Wednesday afternoon, Eric Clapton sat in his front room practising Dobro to background accompaniment supplied by a Don Williams album. Within the last few weeks Clapton had discovered a new hero, digesting a steady diet of the collected Williams vinyl works.

On the surface, this country and western appreciation may seem totally divorced from Clapton's more familiar blues power. But the backbone of country music revolves around the same raw emotions that Clapton exclusively deals with. Pain and anguish hurts plenty in Nashville too.

Clapton studiously picks out a tune on a beautiful handmade Dobro. Several nights back Don Williams and his two man band had raised hell at Eric's, jamming the night away with 'pickin' and drinkin' being the most popular pastimes.

But that merry confrontation was two days ago. Now, in sober daylight, Clapton began to revert to his less confident posture. Having agreed to play Dobro with Williams during several tunes at a London concert, self-doubt and insecurity began to plague the guitarist. Always more of a musician than a personality, Clapton longed to walk onstage at the Hammersmith Odeon stripped of his illustrious past. Oh, to be a sideman stuck behind those anonymous amps once again.

'I spend my time listening to people and being heavily influenced by them,' Clapton said quietly, gently putting down the specially crafted Dobro. 'Then it comes time to record and I go down to the studio, try something new and it comes out as me again.'

The battle between what the public demand and what EC really wants to give them has reached a healthy balance. Clapton does not concern himself with filling any preconceived roles. He always wore the adulation awkwardly anyway. While the masses credited first the Yardbirds and later Cream with defining heavy metal electric playing, Clapton tossed off virtuoso riffs with his back to the audience.

'I don't want to be immodest but I like to attract people to my music and not to anything else. If they don't know who it is and they put the record on and like it, then it means I've succeeded,' he said seriously, 'rather than selling something on the strength of anything else like my name or my legend that built up around me.'

Within the last few years, Clapton has tried to gently defuse the legend. Sitting in his front room looking more like one of the lads than a famous rock 'n' roller, it was hard to believe that all the gold albums that decorated the corridor walls really belonged to him. Maybe this guy with the warm smile and fancy Dobro was really the gardener. Maybe the master of the house was out on tour.

The speakers at one end of the room look more like onstage amplification than the standard at home stereo console. Much of the front room is filled with some sort of musical paraphenalia. Cardboard boxes bursting at the seams are stuffed alphabetically with hundreds of records practically filling one side of the room.

In the corner an impressive antique treasure chest arouses suspicions until its contents are revealed by the proud owner. Inside this pirate chest lay hundreds of albums, now deleted collector's items. EC pulls out an ancient Chuck Berry album with an eye-catching cover of strawberries and giggles. After all, he's just another fan.

Some of his favourite guitars enjoy a seat on the couch. 'They get insecure if I don't give them enough attention,' he said with a grin. Behind the guitars stands a Fender Rhodes piano and next to that a complete drum kit.

'What can I do?' Clapton asked helplessly, still thinking about rolling with Don several nights ago.

'I'm at home here on my own 'cept for the old woman and the dog. It's hard to be influenced, hard to do anything electric. I can't just pick up a guitar and play on my own. So I play acoustic all the time. That's how the songs are written. And it's very difficult to break that mould once you've stepped into it.'

The mould Clapton has craftfully constructed is charged with the same emotional intensity that filled each original classically structured solo. Always an extremely sensitive, romantic sentimentalist, this outpouring of emotions was originally most prominent in his guitar playing. Now similarly intense sentiments abound in his songwriting, singing and acoustic guitar playing. Expect no heavy metal cop-out from this guitarist.

'I don't really think they want a heavy metal album. At least I hope they don't cause they're not gonna get it anymore,' EC said with the utmost determination to uphold his words. 'I'm past that kind of thing. I don't think it lasts.'

Unobtrusively perched atop the bass drum, a cute little teddy bear is less ephemeral than countless current rock stars. The teddy is not a childhood original enjoyed by a boyhood Clapton but a latter day replacement.

'Mine was stabbed and stiched up so many times,' Eric laughs genuinely amused. 'It was the one thing I could take everything out on.'

This new teddy, however, is destined for a long and prosperous lifetime. These days Eric Clapton doesn't need to unleash pent-up frustrations on defenseless teddy bears. These days Eric Clapton doesn't have to prove himself to a public weaned on great expectations. No longer concerned with being the fastest gun in the west, Clapton does not worry about a misinformed public looking to him for something that just isn't there.

'I don't hate people expecting just one thing of me,' Clapton said honestly, lighting a cigarette, 'it's just they don't seem to recognise what that one certain thing is. Just because my exterior changes, fuck,' he sighs slightly exasperated, 'that doesn't mean my insides have changed.'

If anything his insides are more prominent on record and stage than ever before. Low-key acoustic tales of broken hearts contain as much emphatic gut-level emotion as any definitive solo. These days Eric Clapton just wants to be himself. He's certainly earned that privilege.

'If people want that heavy metal thing they can go somewhere else. I'm not in any kind of competition. If they put me onstage with Beck,' he says the word with much respect, 'who's really fast and tough, I'd just have to play rhythm guitar.

'What I'm trying to do is find another way of doing it so it's distinctively me. And if it has to be softer and even unrecognisable at first then that's all right even if it's not the current trend. There's always gonna be some young kid who can do it twice as good as you,' Clapton maturely rationalised. 'So you develop something else, try and stay away from the gun shot and out of the line of fire.'

Resplendent in faded denims, a short sleeve faded tartan shirt, slippers and a just-beginning-to-wake-up look, Eric Clapton stared a half empty bottle of Carlsberg Special Brew in the face. A package of Rothmans lay within easy reach as did a small blue plastic plectrum which read: THIS IS MY FUCKING PICK E.C.

The owner of this specially made plectrum tossed off one of those inimitable smiles that silently speak of sentiments as warm as those he sings about in Hello Old Friend. No longer content to mechanically churn out past achievements, Eric Clapton still wants success. But he wants it strictly on his own terms. All that's shifted is the perspective.

'All that emotion is in the writing now instead of the guitar playing,' he said quietly, confronting the Carlsberg Special Brew with the appreciation of a true connoisseur. 'The important thing to preserve is the emotion rather than technique. I'd like to think my voice is actually as good now as my guitar playing because that should make the right balance.'

Every time Clapton makes another album he gives away more of himself. While the misguided grope desperately for some rock star to lead them down the path of salvation towards the second coming, Clapton is more concerned with honesty and integrity than some clever hot lick.

The Clapton of the seventies is not very removed from the sixties legend. The connection is emotion, now more apparent than ever. While Badge or Born Under a Bad Sign may have previously conjured up visual images while providing astounding musical moments, All Our Past Times or Black Summer Rain from his newest album No Reason to Cry are equally contagious and satisfying.

Creativity and growth is dependent on change and stimulation. Just a couple of one night stands drive the point home. Clapton has to adopt new styles and progressions to maintain his own sanity. Ten years ago Eric Clapton was a very different person than the one sitting on the couch listening to Don Williams today. Ten years ago we were all different. But the past has been intuitively linked with the present by a consistant emotional thread which runs through the bulk of his work.

'If you listen to anybody who's been at it a long time there's always a thread of similarity that goes through each record. There's a track on each record of mine that's almost identical. You can't change that much whatever you try and do. You just change the musicians and the environment around you.'

Critics complain with deep consternation about both the environment and musicians Clapton has chosen, preferring an all-star cast of famous names than a relatively unknown bunch of Tulsa musical freaks. But Clapton is one of the most unorthodox guys around. Maybe someone else needs superstar support to produce magic but Clapton depends on the family atmosphere of love and affection more than technical

slowhand **ERIC CLAPTON** 45

virtuosity.

'Whenever you go into the studio you do whatever the environment seems to suggest. I can't stick to my guns that hard when I've got all those musicians to bend to my will,' he said laconically, taking a hearty swig of the Special Brew. 'It's always got to be a collective idea.

'I have to preserve the integrity between all of us,' Clapton says sincerely, radiating one of those 'smiles'. 'If I recorded an album with some other people our band trust would be abused.'

Clapton enjoys a very special rapport with his band. No longer intimidated by his giant shadow, the band now have the confidence in themselves to step out front with perceptive musical support. This positive sign of encouragement has given Clapton the motivation to tenderly hold the reigns, driving the entire assembly to a Grand Prix finale. No overnight process, it's taken the band three long hard years to grow and get into one cohesive unit.

Last summer Clapton seemed restless and agitated. But previous insecurities no longer dot his conversation. Basically, Clapton is very shy and retiring. Only time and patience can permeate the sensitive surface. And the same qualities must be employed when listening to his recent albums, none of which can be simply dismissed as easy listening. Easy? At times the intensity is frightening.

'It's in the writing now instead of the guitar playing so much. If people can't see the similarity that's

Ok,' he said without a trace of hostility or bitterness. 'It's not something they need to know. They might subconsciously sense it but it's not necessary for me to make it so obvious that they jump up and recognise it.'

He instantly agrees that he is much happier now than last summer.

'Last summer I went through a little period, not of confusion, but indecision. Towards the end of last year there was a lot of friction within the band, several personal vendettas that I found very distracting. I couldn't keep my mind on the direction I was going in because I felt like I had to keep patching things up.

'But that's gone away now,' Clapton flashed a contented grin. 'It's like a family. Everyone knows what they can't tread on. That's made it easier for me to write, play, sing, just everything because now I know I've got total support. Besides they're in debt to me so they can't get away!'

The reasons behind these financial problems are distinctly unusual. The Eric Clapton Band primarily consists of a bunch of Kodak junkies who need to feed their habit especially while on tour. During their recent British tour, Clapton reckons most of the band spent most of their wages on film and film processing. Several have been known to go through Tri-X withdrawal.

'They're mad,' Eric says collapsing with laughter. 'All the money they make on tour goes to developing the photos they take on tour! It works for me 'cause they can't escape. They're in debt to me.'

Clapton's recent British tour was another adventure

in low profile living. While his contemporaries cruise into the country for the odd date at Earl's Court, Clapton stuck to seaside resorts and acoustically sound halls. He works better in situations where pressure and preconceived expectations are kept at a minimum. That was the whole idea upon which Derek and the Dominoes was built.

'I got very annoyed about that tour with Derek and the Dominoes 'cause in some towns, especially in America, we would turn up and it would say DEREK AND THE DOMINOES FEATURING ERIC CLAPTON. I'd call the office and have dreadful rows,' he good humouredly recalls. 'Still it kept happening. Obviously, they wanted to sell the tickets but I didn't want it that way. I just wanted it to be a group for it's own sake.

'The last time I did a tour of England like the one we've just done was with Derek and the Dominoes which was a good while back and we just scraped the road. We did places where you couldn't even put your guitar down,' he says totally bemused. 'But it was fun.'

This summer's British touring lark was no exception. Determined to enjoy himself, Clapton purposely avoided the Earl's Court aircraft hangar syndrome, concentrating instead on more intimate halls.

'Well,' he leans back and laughs, 'I don't think I could fill Earl's Court. It's a pretty big place. I can't imagine a group playing there. I think the only time I've been there was to see the Ideal Home exhibition when I was young. I can't imagine playing a place like that! I'd have to see it as I saw it as a kid with tents, cars

and houses.'

This summer's British jaunt was not void of headline attention. Just another reminder of Clapton's vulnerable honesty, there was the Enoch Powell escapade. Unlike other artistes of his stature, Clapton can't be bothered to disguise true feelings or adopt phony attitudes.

So one night in Birmingham someone said something that triggered off an unexpected part of Clapton's rowdier personality. Maybe it was the drink. Maybe it was just a bad day. But it was so human and typically Eric. How many times have you gotten a bit drunk and spouted out great truths and philosphies only to later blush the next morning?

'I thought it was quite funny actually. I don't know much about politics. I don't even know if it would be good or bad for him to get in. I don't even know who the Prime Minister is now,' he laughs, not entirely serious. 'I just don't know what came over me that night. It must have been something that happened in the day but it came out in this garbled thing,' he laughs at the recollection. 'I'm glad you printed the letter though.

'I thought the whole thing was like Monty Python. There's this rock group playing onstage and the singer starts talking about politics. Great,' Clapton leans back and laughs.

'It's so stupid. Those people who paid their money sittin' listening to this madman dribbling on and the band meanwhile getting fidgety thinking 'oh, dear'.'

And you were going to quit rock 'n' roll and run for a constituency in Surrey, I remind him as he begins to

laugh uncontrollably.

'I don't even know if we've got an MP in Surrey! I guess I should be expecting a letter from Enoch Powell any day now. Could get a libel suit as well 'cause I said he was the only politician mad enough to run the country. I didn't use his full name though,' Eric says like an innocent schoolboy, 'so it could be Enoch anybody. I don't even know what sparked it off.'

Probably the Arabs I jestingly offer.

'Oh, that's ok,' EC muses. 'I think they don't know how to spend their money. They're buying things for completely over the top prices without knowing it. I'm sure they're being taken left, right and centre. But they're sinking a lot of money into England and we'll probably regain it if we're clever enough. Then they'll have to go back and discover more oil.'

Before returning to a more musical conversation, EC spins an entertaining vingette about a friend who was staying at the Dorchester. Apparently some rich Arab pointed to Hyde Park and enquired about the asking price.

Owning Hyde Park is not one of Eric Clapton's lifetime ambitions. He is more concerned with grooming his band into a tightly run, spontaneous organisation. After years of disdain about running a band, his newly discovered self-confidence has made him an excellent skipper.

'I'll tell ya something about that. I been watching Stan Kenton's schedule for the last three to four years. He's a trumpeter who leads a 30 piece band,' EC mumbles in disbelief, finishing off another Special Brew. 'He works every night, two weeks off at Christmas. When you look at something like that you've got no reason to cry, no reason to complain about anything when you see someone at that age doing it for the pure love of it.'

That remains Clapton's idea of musical Utopia, playing for genuine love and enjoyment. Almost every time EC finds himself in a multi-million dollar super-group, he immediately retreats back into hibernation.

'The problem is you grow to hate the rock business. That's why I always have to keep putting myself in situations where I can just enjoy it and not think about the business side 'cause I hate that.

'It's very much the old pals act. That's why I don't go into London much. You go from one office to the next and they're all just bitchin' about each other. Who do you believe?' he asks slightly confused. 'I just come back here and get back in the cocoon. Bugger them all. I just live for the art of making good music, not filling their pockets.'

His obvious disdain for the business side of rock tends means that Clapton depends on his management and record company run by Robert Stigwood.

'The best things always happen by accident,' Clapton says sincerely, giving away one of his ten commandments. 'I trust in that more than deliberate plan. This band I've got was an accident. I'm very lucky I'm with the organisation I am because I get totally free rein.

'I'm never told to do anything. I'm asked or things are suggested but I can say no. I can't imagine working for some conglomerate where they just tell you that you have radio interviews today and Russell Harty tomorrow.'

Eric Clapton does not like to be pigeon holed. He won't arrive back in this country and make outlandish statements about the tax while posing for the story to run in tomorrow's Daily Mail. Eric Clapton is the total antithesis of the music business machine filmed for posterity on BBC2's recent Rod Stewart documentary. The only public place you're likely to find Clapton is down the pub.

'It's the motivation that's important. There's a lot of people I see who make records and won't exploit themselves onstage. There was a group I wanted to take on our British tour but they refused to do it. And I think that was because they didn't want the exposure,' Eric says with admiration. 'They were songwriters and they didn't want to get boosted to the point where they didn't have the time to write songs anymore. They just wanted to stay where they were.'

The group turns out to be Gallagher and Lyle, two songwriters for whom Clapton has the utmost respect. Like the 'Breakaway' duo, Eric Clapton wears his heart on his sleeve.

What he exposes now on record and in conversation is a very healthy and vibrant self-portrait. As Eric is quick to admit, the playing is the one constant factor. It's his personality make-up which has gone through a positive about-face.

'With the last album I've put myself back into that situation where a lot of people think I'm playing guitar on every track. I've done another Derek And The Dominoes and haven't listed who's playing what on each track. In actual fact I only play lead guitar on two tracks. The rest is little guests,' he fiendishly chuckles. 'Now they have to guess which one's me. And I'm not gonna tell.'

No longer confined to fulfilling guitar gaps, Clapton has taken advantage of this freedom. The days of every track containing a definitive guitar solo belong to the past. And as Clapton is quick to stress in song 'all our past times must be forgotten'.

'Quite honestly I don't think I could play one of those solos on every track. My lead guitar playing has really slipped because I'm controlling the band, writing songs, everything else. Consequently something has to suffer and the lead guitar has probably suffered most of all.'

For the majority of his earlier career, lead guitar was EC's only concern and mainline function.

'That was all I had to worry about then,' he recalls signalling to Patti that it's time for another round of Carlsberg. 'All I had to do was get up in the morning, go to the gig and play lead guitar.'

Being one of the original guitar heroes, most of the staff here curiously wanted to know what EC thought about his modern day counterparts. Like other reliable sixties mainstays, Clapton listens to old and new influences. Of the new, Don Williams, Gallagher & Lyle and a new artiste, Stephen Bishop, dominate over the latest effort from Robin Trower.

'I thought Mick Ronson was very good on the telly the other night,' Clapton smiles referring to the Whistle Test Dylan special. 'It was so obvious he was an English guitarist with the old guitar down here, down to his knees,' Clapton laughs. 'I don't listen to clever lead guitar playing anymore. I'm more interested in total songs.

'To be quite honest I haven't heard Robin Trower. Blackmore? He probably suffers from the fact that he's had to live up to his own image too. I bet that must bother him a lot,' EC reflects, strongly relating to the situation.

'The first time I saw Blackmore I think he was playing with Johnny Kidd. He floored me then. Later I saw him at the Roundhouse with Deep Purple and he'd stepped out of being just a good sideman and into a heavy number. Now he's living with it.'

Rather than exploit his previous guitar star stance, Clapton has chosen to live without any nasty crosses that demand attention bearing. Unfortunately, his audience is not as eager to step forward. Still, progress marches on.

'I think my audience now is probably the same one I've had all along only they're probably very disgruntled because I keep laying new tricks on them and they're really not sure if they want to accept them or not.'

The key to the 'new' Clapton revolves around simplicity, stuffed with genuine emotions.

'I was talkin' to Don Williams the other night about being able to write a song where halfway through the listener will know the end and be able to sing along. I don't want people to sit down and listen to my album really hard 20 times to find out what I'm saying,' Clapton says adamantly. 'I'd like to make it as simple as possible.

'I'm sure there will always be a circuit. There will always be somewhere to play,' says this musician bent on a long career. 'I'm in the musician's union. I could get a job playin' for the BBC. There's no panic.

'That's what I see in a lot of the groups today, this sort of mad panic; gotta get a number one, then do the TVs. It's like they expect their careers to end in three years,' he laughs in disbelief, 'Everyone is so busy trying to think of new approaches to catch the eye and it doesn't really matter 'cause it's all been done before.'

And much of what's been done before has been done to perfection by Clapton himself. Understandably, he's a little itchy to start moving in another direction. Not until the flittering presence of Blind Faith did a gentler side of Clapton begin to flourish.

With Delaney & Bonnie, and later with the Dominoes, Clapton began to explore the land of one thousand Dobros and acoustic guitar tunings, encouraged and stimulated by Duane Allman.

What really changed Clapton's musical perspective was the discovery of the Band. In a previous interview last summer he admitted that when Big Pink came out his entire conception of Cream changed drastically.

Suddenly, Cream seemed more like a con than the authentic music the Band spun.

'The Band had a great effect on me. I'd never really liked country music. I always thought it was oversentimental. This is when I was into being very aggressive and playing just straight blues. Country music was just sloppy,' he grins. 'But the Band bridged the gap. The Byrds got there quite early. But the Band gave it a bite that country music just didn't seem to have before.

'I wasn't even that big a Dylan fan till Like a Rolling Stone. Wait a minute, I did buy an album The Times They Are a Changin' and sat down and learned it straight away. See the trouble is that people expect electric music from me. If I go to a session I take an electric guitar because it's second nature to me. But lately,' he says, pleased with recent changes, 'the Dobro has taken up all my time.'

When he isn't playing Dobro, EC spends his time listening to Don Williams. That's his passion this week. In between rounds of Special Brew, Eric gets up and puts on a tape Williams recorded at his house the other night. EC reclines into the caverns of the sofa and listens to this euphoric music.

Clapton first saw Don Williams on an American chat show, the Dinah Shore Show. This interview programme is so lacking in any perceptions that it serves as a nationwide vehicle for slick PR campaigns. But EC was impressed with this character. After singing a song, Williams joined Dinah and her other guests,

slowhand **ERIC CLAPTON** | **55**

ERIC CLAPTON slowhand

62 **ERIC CLAPTON** slowhand

refusing to join in with the trivial conversation. Clapton was impressed.

When a British Don Williams tour was announced, EC was among the first to order tickets for the opening night in Croydon. Pleased that they met on even ground, neither artiste was totally familiar with the other. Within several weeks they became good friends. Another example of the Clapton personality: he prefers starting relationships on a firm footing void of past preconceived ideas. For all the assertive point making, Eric Clapton really is a new artiste.

Nevertheless, he has retained certain personality traits. Despite total backing and encouragement from the Don Williams Band, Clapton was nervous and hesitant about appearing at the Hammersmith Odeon. Assured that the crowd would belong strictly to Williams, familar insecurities bothered his conscience. 'I haven't had to practise in so long,' he said looking sheepishly at the Dobro.

Suddenly Clapton jumps up and discovers that he is very hungry. In the kitchen, where the refrigerator is decorated with various backstage passes and the walls covered with summer tour posters, Patti is impressively concocting some homemade scotch eggs. 'Hurry UP,' Eric jests, 'I'm STARVING.'

Moments later the scotch eggs are ready, which calls for another round of Carlsberg. Eric puts on a cassette of the debut album from Stephen Bishop, a songwriter Clapton did some sessions for and surprisingly found himself loving the material.

'He's got the best range I've heard in years,' Eric enthused between bites of salad. 'Joni Mitchell can't get anywhere near that! Woody's manager asked me to do the session and I thought it was a joke. I called his bluff and it was real!

'What attracted me most was not knowing what you were stepping into and finding that it was very good. I don't get asked to do sessions very often so I thought it was a joke.'

Thriving in a pressure-free situation, Clapton enjoyed the sessions as much as he enjoyed his Don Williams encounters. In these two instances he was allowed to escape from his legend. He wasn't (sigh gasp shock) Eric Clapton, he was simply a musician.

'I'm always more comfortable in situations like that,' Eric said recalling the low-key atmosphere at his holiday camp gig. 'The pressures are off and I feel comfortable because there is no-one to prove myself to.'

For his most recent album, Clapton surrounded himself with the best. In addition to his own able-bodied band, he enjoyed contributions from Bob Dylan, Ron Wood and the Band. The project worked because, like everything else EC does, it all happened accidentally.

Using Shangri-La studios, most of the Band were hovering around the sessions as it's their home base. Even before going to LA, Clapton worked out with some relaxation in Nassau.

'Woody came to stay at this house we were renting. He was pushing me around trying to get me to write songs but I couldn't do it in that situation 'cause it was too idyllic. We finally wrote a couple songs that we didn't use. One was called You're Too Good To Die You Should Be Buried Alive. Can you believe that?' he asks incredulously. 'It's all there in the files. All these crazy songs.'

Armed with a bunch of songs and not much of an idea about album direction, EC and Woody headed for Shangri-La. Much to Clapton's delightful surprise everything eventually gelled.

'I was in a situation where people were coming to visit me. It wasn't so much 'Ah, the BAND' it was just people who came to visit. Some of the jams were amazing because they hadn't played together in ages. There were hundreds of guitars. On my birthday party it was the first time the entire Band played together in a long time.

'Richard Manuel and I are like blood brothers. Every night when the session ended we'd be the only one's left standing. We'd just play all fuckin' night,' Clapton enthuses.

'On the first tour we did with EC And The Jordinaires, the Band made me get up and play on Chest Fever. I could never understand the words and it turned out nor could they. They kept singing different lines. All I had to do was get up there and play guitar and sing the first thing that came into my head,' he recalls in amusement. 'There was this incredible sound of voices in many tongues saying different things.'

Clapton proceeds to relate an entertaining tale about recording All Our Past Times where Rick Danko kept singing his verse differently each take, much to Clapton's amusement and confusion.

'Dylan is another one like that. He can't restrict himself to any one way of doing a song so we did Sign Language three times. I thought fuck it, I'll just go as loose as he is. I'm used to doing a song one way but Dylan throws caution to the wind every time.'

That seemed most apparent on the recent TV concert Hard Rain.

'Yeah, and it looked like nobody else knew what he was gonna do either. He kept turning round as if to say 'this is what's gonna happen next'. The band must have been ready for anything to happen.'

Clapton indulges in similar onstage conduct which consistantly makes for a fresh and spontaneous atmosphere. None too fond of musical claustrophobia, EC detests boredom.

'Sure we do that and it's very confusing for the rest of the band. But you can't play the same thing every night the same way because then you really get to hate it. I think we did Layla one night in 3/4 time,' Clapton laughs hysterically. 'It sounded great. Just like a good old waltz.'

Assuming the main Layla riff immortalised the song forever, many of Clapton's more recent efforts have been built around similarly addicting backbones, only the acoustic groove might be too subtle to instantly digest.

'Should I tell you where I got that riff from,' Eric says

in animation, beginning to enjoy himself. 'It's an Albert King riff off an album called Born Under a Bad Sign and there's a song called There Is Nothing I Can Do if You Leave Me Here to Cry,' he sings the line in sleepy time sounding a bit like Smile.

'Duane heard that and just went,' Eric starts to hum the main Layla theme. 'He just speeded it up. Then we took to doing Layla in the studio and then that particular song afterwards. No-one would notice that the riff is exactly the same except slow blues. Really good trick that.'

Suddenly EC jumps up again and goes to the albums treasure chest in search of the Albert King record. Pointing to the chest and all the cardboxes on the floor Clapton says in disbelief, 'And you ask me my ten favourite songs! Look how many I've got to choose from.'

What with all the Carlsberg Special Brews, a visit to the lavatory is necessary. This small room is decorated with an unusual assortment of postcards from round the world. There's one cartoon of two little creatures talking. One says 'Is it true that sex pins your hearing?' While the other replies 'Beg pardon?'. And there's a tacky but charming card of two birds with the loving inscription 'Thanks for the Budgie'.

Back to business. No Reason To Cry, unlike his recent albums, was not produced by Tom Dowd. The reasons behind this were mostly political as RSO had moved distribution in America to Polydor from Atlantic and WEA threw a boycott on Dowd producing Clapton.

This might have been a blessing in disguise. Even during the making of There's One In Every Crowd Clapton disagreed at times with the clinical approach Dowd sometimes favoured, preferring a live atmosphere.

After a few beers, Clapton's conversation becomes more animated, honest and relaxed. 'The thing that bothered me about There's One in Every Crowd was that we were contriving to make a quality record. Tom kept getting serious about 'making a record' when we were having a good time. Like Pretty Blue Eyes was done in bits of something like six bars here and there which is a frustrating way to record.

'I prefer to work live whenever possible. And No Reason to Cry was pretty live. Fortunately or unfortunately, whichever it turns out to be, we didn't use Tom Dowd again. Robert said I had to make an album as soon as possible. Not being able to use Tom just threw me,' EC recalls in panic. 'It threw me into a trauma. I thought of Robbie Robertson but he was busy doing Neil Diamond.'

With a tendency to be lazy, I wondered if Clapton needed gentle prodding from Robert Stigwood to record.

'Yeah, it is good. After a couple of days recording I was walkin' round the studio saying 'I'm packin' it in, I don't want any more to do with it'. It was my fault because I said all right to Robert and he came back with a bloody deadline! I called his bluff,' Eric laughs, 'and he came back with a bloody deadline.

'Usually Robert would say 'if you don't want to do it fine' but it was all to do with that year I spent out of the country. As it happens the album turned out well – much to the surprise of everyone 'cause we walked in loathing the idea. If it hadn't been for the outside jollity of the Band we wouldn't have gotten anything done. We were stuck.

'If I go into the studio with my band they're gonna look to me for something to do and I had nothing,' Eric winces at the memory. 'Richard Manuel came up with Beautiful Thing and from there we just went. It was something to do.'

Clapton is exaggerating when he says he had 'nothing'. Still somewhat insecure about his songwriting ability, he will only present the very best to the band for close inspection.

'Worried? God, you don't know what it's like. We took two weeks off to reconsider the whole thing. I just thought 'God, it's all fallen down'. That's how Black Summer Rain came about. Then I thought, 'well that's not a bad song', took it back and it kicked like mad.

'It's one thing to play to an audience you don't know and can't see but it's always been very difficult for me to play a song to someone I know face to face who has good taste in music.'

From the album, Clapton is satisfied personally with Hello Old Friend, All Our Past Times and Black Summer Rain, three of the album's best moments, all written by EC. His songwriting is rapidly improving and perfecting. The next hit single could well be an honest,

Pictorial Press

gentle representation of EC 1976.

'The songs you write very quickly are always the best. The ones that are written in the space of a day. It's like this new one I just wrote after we came back from that Buddy Holly luncheon. It was just about taking the old woman out and getting too sloshed to drive home. It was perfect,' he grins proudly.

Anxious to get the song down on tape as quickly as possible, Clapton plays a demo version recorded with Ronnie Lane at his house. Entitled You Look Wonderful Tonight it's one of the most beautiful love songs I've ever heard. The lyrics are equally sensitive and real, apparently about a conversation Eric and Patti have every time they go out. Just from two listenings, I've been singing the song all week. It also happens to be extremely sexy.

Future plans remain both concrete and tenuous but one thing is certain: Clapton is determined to have a good time. Later this month he leaves for a three-week American tour and hopes to record the next album immediately after the tour in Nashville.

'I really wanna get down to Nashville,' he said glancing quickly at the Dobro. 'It's not very far from Tulsa. Can't be more than twenty-four hours.'

That project belongs to the concrete. An album of pub songs belongs to the tenuous. Those might even be recorded in a pub. And there's a possible musical adventure on the cards between EC and Ronnie Lane. Besides, he could always work for the BBC.

'I'm actually gonna form a group called 'The Hypocrites' with Ronnie Lane,' Eric says with much laughter. 'Aw, I've given it away. We'll record on our own label called 'Get Away With Murder Records'. The first gig is at the Cranleigh Village Hall.'

Visions of ploughing matches dance through my head, I laugh.

'This is true,' EC insists. 'No lie. The first gig is at the Cranleigh Village Hall.'

Somewhere in between the concrete and the tenuous, Clapton wants his next single to be that new love song. Regardless, it's definitely going on the next album and it's definitely one of the best songs he's ever written, sort of the antithesis to Layla.

'It's funny ya know 'cause I didn't even want I Shot The Sheriff on the album. Didn't even want it out at all. I thought it was a rip-off,' he says in animated Carlsberg tones. 'I had to live with this till this very day – Eric goes reggae! Then they follow it up with another bloody reggae song. Oh, dear. Branded again.'

You lose one cross and gain another. But last summer's self-doubt has been replaced by well-nourished confidence. Clapton seems to believe in his music now more than ever. Even last summer when he talked of making a rock 'n' roll album, he never seemed convinced.

'If you remember that was after There's One in Every Crowd didn't make it so I thought 'oh, well,' Eric recalls the point when he was on the brink of making artistic concessions and selling himself short.

'In fact I did put out a rock album more or less with

EC Was Here which maybe covered that for a little while, filling up that space I was complaining about. If the album had horns on, it would have been perfect for hard rock. So now,' he smiles shyly, 'I've got time to be myself again.

'I want to do an album where every song says something that relates to my life. I've got some songs down that are getting that way,' he concluded humming a bit of that contagious new love song. 'I'd like a hit single but I wouldn't want to make a living that way.'

With every album Clapton becomes more comfortable and more confident with himself. It is no accident that the best tracks are always Clapton originals. Wait till you hear You Look Wonderful Tonight. The song is so good EC will give Gallagher & Lyle some heavy competition.

'Oh dear,' Eric sighs with a long yawn, reclining into the couch, 'I'm exhausted.'

And rightfully so. For several hours now he was Eric Clapton again. Little man you've had a busy day.

EC'S TOP TEN

1) Drown In My Own Tears by Ray Charles

He recorded it two ways, live and in the studio. The live one is great. I like it very much.

2) Pretend by Carl Mann

It's very old. He did a record called Mona Lisa that Conway Twitty had a hit with. But Carl Mann did the original and he did another one called Pretend. (He begins to sing) 'Pretend you're happy when you're

blue'. It's sorta like Smile only rocked up with a really nice guitar part.

3) Help Yourselves To Each Other by Don Williams

That's a new favourite of mine. It's got really nice words and a pleasant melody. No you can't dance to it. It's just mesmerising.

4) Stevie Wonder Presents Syreeta and Syreeta.

I'm not sure which album is better. Stevie Wonder produced them and they're both good. Then nothing happened. She had one hit off the second album Spinning and Spinning.

5) Chirping Crickets

That was the first album I ever bought. And it still plays after all these years. I have records I've had for only six months that don't play anymore. Chirping Crickets I've had since I was 16. Buddy Holly's first album. I learned the whole thing straight away. I couldn't believe it. It was the first time I'd seen a Stratocaster as well. He's standing on the cover holding a Stratocaster and I thought 'what is that space vehicle'.

6) Bridge Over Troubled Water by Stevie Wonder

It's from a live album Live At The Talk Of The Town which I think is only available in this country. You should hear it. He slows it right down. The dynamics are very heavy. It builds up and comes down to almost silence. He used an amazing bass player who ended up playing with Miles Davis.

7) Caress Me Baby by Jimmy Reed

That was the first time I heard really low, low down

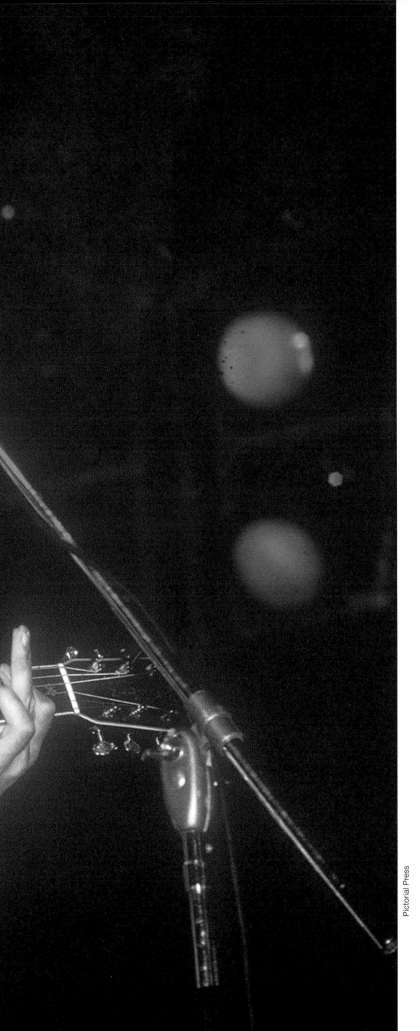

R&B. They released it as a single in this country. I probably heard that before I even heard Muddy Waters. It's on the album Rockin' With Reed.

8) Loving You Is Sweeter Than Ever by Stevie Wonder

Well, he wrote it. It's a great song. Four Tops did it too. The Band recorded it but never released it. They do it like they do that Marvin Gaye song Baby Don't You Do It. Rick Danko sings a great vocal.

9) Willowy Garden

It's a traditional song, a Scots melody. I don't really know the words to that except for the first verse. I wrote off to Cecil Sharpe House who've got the words to every song ever written, especially folk songs. I got the words and couldn't bloody understand it cause it's written in old English. It's an old pub song. People usually make up their own words for the verse but the chorus is always the same. It goes back centuries.

10) Little Man You've Had A Busy Day

That's the oldest song I know 'cause it used to rock me to sleep. Someone like Al Bowlly might have done it. The words go 'Someone stole your marbles I know what I'll do/Dad will buy some new ones/Time to go to sleep now/Little man you've had a busy day'. (He sings in lullaby fashion.) It's one of my favourite songs. It used to knock me out. That's why I don't know it well. I'd never get to hear the last verse 'cause I'd be asleep.

© BARBARA CHARONE, 1976

ERIC CLAPTON:
any objections?

(BARBARA CHARONE, CREEM, FEBRUARY 1977)

If home is where the heart is, then Eric Clapton hides his emotions inside a sprawling countryside retreat aptly named Hurtwood Edge. The name of this peaceful sanctuary reveals more about Eric Clapton than any compilation album stuffed with breathtaking guitar solos. Despite the warm domestic tranquillity, the living room still looks like a rehearsal room. Clapton studiously picks out a tune on a beautifully crafted Dobro.

A Don Williams album blasts out of speakers that look more like lethal onstage amplification than your usual home stereo console. Wearing a hazy, just-beginning-to-wake-up-look, Clapton stared a half empty bottle of beer in the face. He gently puts the Dobro down on the couch and sighs restlessly. 'What can I do?' he says in frustration, 'I'm at home here on my own 'cept for the old lady and the dog. It's hard to be influenced, hard to do any electric. I can't just pick up an electric guitar and play on my own. So I play acoustic all the time. That's how the songs are written. And it's difficult to break that mould once you've stepped into it.'

Cardboard boxes burst at the seams with hundreds of records that spill over into an antique chest, testifying to his diverse musical preferences. Some of his favourite guitars share a seat on the couch. Behind Clapton, a complete drum kit and a Fender Rhodes piano beg for attention. Mysteriously perched atop the bass drum, a cuddly teddy bear waits patiently. Like his last three studio albums, the teddy belongs to a new mould totally divorced from Clapton's adolescent past.

slowhand **ERIC CLAPTON** 75

'Mine was stabbed and stitched up so many times,' Eric laughs in bemused recollection. 'It was the only thing I could take everything out on.'

That was before he discovered the electric guitar as a useful vehicle for unleashing pent-up frustrations. Never stabbed nor stitched, this new teddy is destined for a healthy lifetime.

No longer treading that thin line between public demands and private priorities, Clapton's personal battles have reached a healthy impasse. Now he's got room to breathe.

'I spend my time listening to people and being heavily influenced by them,' Clapton says as Don Williams plays on. 'Then when it comes time to record, I go down to the studio, try something new, and it comes out as me again.

'I don't want to be immodest but I like to attract people to my music and not to anything else. If they don't know who it is and they put the record on and like it, then it means I've succeeded rather than selling something on the strength of my name or the legend that has built up around me.'

Always more a musician than a personality, from his first stint with the Yardbirds, the retiring guitarist who turned his back on sold-out Cream audiences prefers anonymity to the spotlight. That was the whole premise upon which Derek and the Dominoes was initially built.

'I got very annoyed during our American tour when we would turn up and it would say Derek And The Dominoes Featuring Eric Clapton, I'd call the office and have dreadful rows. Obviously they wanted to sell the tickets but I just wanted it to be a group for it's own sake.'

When Layla was first released, no-one really knew that Derek was Eric. Once his identity surfaced, adulation and acclaim grew in such large proportions that Clapton quickly adopted a lifestyle based around hibernation and public withdrawal.

'All the emotion is in the writing now instead of the guitar playing,' EC says emphatically, finishing off the first of many beers. 'The important thing to preserve is the emotion rather than the technique. If you listen to anybody who's been at it a long time there's always a thread of similarity that runs through each record.

'I don't mind people expecting just one thing of me, it's just that they don't recognize what that one certain thing is. Just 'cause my exterior changes, fuck!' he sighs in exasperation. 'That doesn't mean my insides have changed.'

'If people want that heavy metal thing they can go somewhere else. I'm not in any kind of competition. If they put me onstage with Beck,' he says in reverence with small pangs of insecurity, 'who's really fast and tough, I'd just have to play rhythm guitar.

'What I'm trying to do is find another way of making music that's distinctly me. And if it has to be softer and even unrecognisable at first then that's all right, even if it's not the current trend. There's always gonna be some young kid who can do it twice as good as you. So you develop something else, try and stay away from the line of fire.'

No longer concerned with being the fastest gun in the West, Clapton speaks maturely from a wounded past. Rather than mechanically repeat previous accomplishments - it's taken three years of natural growing pains to free himself from his lead guitar bondage with his American band, he has taken full advantage of this freedom.

'Quite honestly I don't think I could play one of those solos on every track. My lead guitar playing has slipped because I'm controlling the band, writing songs, everything else. Consequently something has to suffer and the lead guitar playing has probably suffered most of all.

'I don't listen to clever lead guitar playing any more. I'm more interested in total songs. The trouble is people expect electric music from me. If I go to a session I take an electric guitar because it's second nature to me. But lately,' he smiles, quite pleased with the transition, 'the Dobro has taken up all my time.'

The Dobro is not exactly a radical departure for Clapton. He explored the realms of that instrument, trading motel shot licks with Duane Allman, in the studio with both Delaney and Bonnie and later the Dominoes. Renewed interest in Dobro-flavored anguish has made him Don Williams' biggest fan.

Finally, beginning to wake up, Clapton jumps up, almost knocking the handmade Dobro on the floor. He charges over to the stereo and selects a tape recorded at home, at Hurtwood Edge, with Williams and band.

Clapton first spied Williams on the tacky Dinah Shore Show and was impressed both with the music and with the fact that Williams refused to indulge in idle gossip with Dinah and the other guests. Clapton himself would have behaved in a similarly introverted fashion.

During a recent British tour, Eric joined Don Williams onstage in London for some fancy Dobro pickin'. Haunted by memories of self doubt, EC brought along friends Pete Townshend and Ronnie Lane for encouragement. Ambling onstage in faded, patched jeans, Clapton cherished this pressure-free opportunity: when big Don announced his special guest, one girl screamed. Two thirds of the orthodox country crowd had never heard of Clapton.

'I'm always more comfortable in situations like that,' Clapton said honestly, opening another beer. 'The pressures are off and I feel comfortable because there is no one to prove myself to.'

More than anything else, Clapton longs to be one of the band. Given the chance to escape from his legend with Don Williams, he wasn't Eric Clapton, he was simply a musician.

Shy and retiring, Clapton never wanted to be God anyway. He always wore the adulation awkwardly. Right now he's more concerned with musical enjoyment than sales figures. Bent on a long career, he talks enthusiastically about one day playing down at the local pub.

'I don't want people to sit down and listen to my

78 | **ERIC CLAPTON** slowhand

album really hard 20 times to find out what I'm saying,' he stressed. 'I'd like to make it as simple as possible. There will always be somewhere to play. I'm in the musicians' union. I could get a job playin' for the BBC. There's no panic.

'That's what I see in a lot of groups today, this sort of mad panic; gotta get a number one, then do the TVs. It's like they expect their careers to end in three years,' he laughs is disbelief. 'Everyone is so busy trying to think of new approaches to catch the eye and it doesn't really matter 'cause it's all been done before.'

And much of what's done before has been done to perfection by Clapton himself. He has been given mass media credit for having defined modern day electric guitar playing.

'I think my audience now is probably the same one I've had all along only they're very disgruntled that I keep laying new tricks on them and they're not really sure if they want to accept them. The best things happen by accident. I trust in that more than deliberate plan.'

All this conversation has made Clapton's normally reticent speech patterns lively and animated. The beer has also whetted his appetite. He jumps up from the couch and heads for the kitchen, passing a clutch of gold albums in the corridor.

In the kitchen, his main inspiration is busy being domestic and fixing some food. 'Hurry up,' Clapton chides Patti Boyd, 'I'm starving.' The refrigerator door is decorated with various backstage passes. Patti and Eric giggle as I point to a poster pic of Clapton above which has been pasted a newspaper headline which asks the thousand dollar question: 'Does This Man Look Worried?' This is not the behavior of troubled souls.

Over food and another round of potent British beer, Eric and Patti tell amusing tales of C&W visits from the Don Williams crew. The raw emotion that lies at the roots of country music hypnotises Clapton.

What drastically altered his musical frame of reference was his discovery of the Band. Upon hearing their debut album Music From Big Pink, Clapton decided that Cream was 'a con'. The homespun authenticity of the Band was more attractive than Cream concoctions of strange brews: 'I'd never really liked country music before because I thought it was over-sentimental,' he says as Patti attentively listens. 'That was when I was into being very aggressive and just playing straight blues. Country music was just sloppy. But the Band bridged the gap. They gave country music a bite it didn't have before.'

Clapton was not content with a taste. He wanted a whole mouthful. After a memorably short-lived stint with superstar ego clashes driven by Blind Faith, Clapton ran off with the support group Delaney and Bonnie and Friends. Some of the friends soon became Dominoes. Then there was a period of silence.

An eerie hush surrounded Hurtwood Edge. His lengthy 'retirement' was not merely the case of too many drugs. He had overdosed on the big business machinery behind superstar rock.

'The problem is you grow to hate the rock business. That's why I always have to keep putting my situations where I can enjoy it. That's why I don't go into London much. You go from one office to another and they're all bitchin' about each other. Who do you believe?

'I just come back here and in the cocoon. Bugger them all. I just live for the art of making good music, not filling anyone's pockets.'

Over a year ago, Clapton talked about a rock 'n' roll album. Not totally convinced, he was on the brink of making artistic concessions to an impatient audience crying out for rock 'n' roll.

'In fact I did put out a rock album more or less with EC Was Here which maybe covered that for a while, filling that space it was complaining about. If the album had horns on it, it would have been perfect for hard rock. So now,' he smiles shyly, 'I've got time to be myself again.'

Clapton needed some prodding to record a new studio album, his first since There's One In Every Crowd. Manager, Robert Stigwood, supplied deadlines and Ron Wood tried to provide directional guidance.

'Woody came to stay with us in Nassau. He was pushing me around trying to get me to write songs but I couldn't because the situation was too idyllic. We finally wrote a couple songs that we didn't use. One was called You're Too Good To Die You Should Be Buried Alive.' He laughs uncontrollably. 'Can you believe that?'

While the Nassau retreat begged for workless enjoyment, the initial atmosphere which permeated the Los Angeles No Reason To Cry sessions was one of chaos and confusion. Clapton started to write.

'After a couple of days I was walkin' round the studio saying I'm packin' it in, I don't want any more to do with it.' Much to the surprise of everyone the album turned out well but we walked in loathing the idea.

'If I go in the studio with my band they're gonna look to me for something and I had nothing,' Clapton playfully winces. 'Richard Manuel came up with Beautiful Thing and from there we just went!'

Visions of Big Pink danced in his head. Using the Band's homebase, Shangri-la Studios, Clapton surrounded himself with his own able-bodied Oklahoma outfit, along with Wood, the Band, and Bob Dylan. The old Clapton who used to stab teddy bears would have been inhibited and withdrawn.

Even as late as August '75, Clapton displayed reticent studio behaviour during a Dylan Desire session. With several guitarists rolling with Bob, Clapton stuck to the corner, strumming the odd rhythm. By March of '76, familiar insecurities were replaced by self-nourished confidences.

'I was in a situation where people were coming to visit me,' he says of this accidental twist of fate. 'It wasn't so much 'Ah, the Band' it was just people who came to visit. Some of the jams were amazing because the Band hadn't played together in ages.'

A funky, plaintive direction gradually evolved. Between Rick Danko and Dylan, Clapton gave up trying to bring the proceedings to order and loosely rolled with the flow.

'Dylan can't restrict himself to one way of doing a song so we did Sign Language three ways. I thought, 'Fuck it, I'm just as loose as he is'. I'm used to doing a song one way but Dylan throws caution to the wind every time.'

Onstage, Clapton indulges in similarly spontaneous conduct. 'You can't play the same song every night the same way because you really get to hate it. I think we did Layla one night in 3/4 time,' Clapton laughs. 'It sounded like a good old waltz.'

As it happens, the song's origins are not as removed from a waltz as one would imagine.

'Should I tell you where I got that riff?' Eric says excitedly, now enjoying himself with help from the beer. 'It's an Albert King riff off an album Born Under A Bad Sign and there's a song called There Is Nothing I Can Do If You Leave Me Here To Cry. Duane Allman heard that and just went!'

He has employed a few tricks on No Reason To Cry as well. Like the Derek and the Dominoes album, Clapton makes the listener discover just which guitar is his.

In retrospect he feels There's One In Every Crowd suffered from a 'contrived' approach and much prefers the live atmosphere which permeates No Reason To Cry. Not surprisingly, the album's best tracks are Clapton originals.

Stranded in between British and American tours, Clapton was stuck inside Hurtwood with those mobile blues again. Restless to play, he kept busy writing songs. One new tune, You Look Wonderful Tonight, is almost an acoustic, antithesis to Layla. A sensual love song written about 'taking the old woman out and getting too sloshed to drive home,' Clapton can't wait to record it. Already he's done a demo with Ronnie Lane.

After the American fall tour, Clapton hopes to record the next album in Nashville, no doubt inspired by his recent Don Williams encounter. 'I really want to get down to Nashville,' he grins, glancing quickly at the idle Dobro. 'It can't be very far from Tulsa. Can't be more than 24 hours.'

Gradually stripping away layers of protective covering and revealing more of himself, Eric Clapton will one day have a hit single that refuses to make any concessions.

'I never even wanted I Shot The Sheriff on the album – I didn't want it out at all. I thought it was a rip-off. To this very day I have to live with 'Eric goes reggae',' he says with more humor than hostility. 'Then they follow it up with another bloody reggae song. Oh, dear. Branded again.'

You lose one cross and you gain another. He may never record another Sunshine of Your Love but you can bet he'll take a bluesy visit down desolation row on every album and in each concert. After all, there's no panic. He could always work for the BBC.

'I'm sure there will always be a circuit,' says this card-carrying member of the musicians' union. 'I've been watching Stan Kenton's schedule for the last three years. He's a trumpet player who leads a 30 piece band! And he works every night of the year with only two weeks off for Christmas. When you see someone that age doing it for the pure love of the music, you've got no reason to cry.'

© BARBARA CHARONE, 1977

Pictorial Press

ERIC CLAPTON *slowhand*

ERIC CLAPTON:
portrait of the artist as a working man

(CHRIS WELCH, MELODY MAKER, 9 DECEMBER 1978)

That whole thing about me talking about Enoch was that it occurred to me that he was the only bloke who was telling the truth, for the good of the country… I believe he is a very religious man. And you can't be religious and racist at the same time. The two things are incompatible.'

It has often been said that one of Eric Clapton's major problems over the years has been to find his own identity, a role in which he can be comfortable and assured. He has been through the most historically important groups of our time, undergone the pressures of an extraordinary fame, given himself up to all the excesses of the rock 'n' roll life-style, been close to death, known misery and oblivion, and come out of it with his talent and sanity intact.

Eric has appeared in many guises: the eager, flippant art school kid with the Yardbirds, the macho blues man with John Mayall, even a psychedelic hippie with Cream in the age of pink boots and frizzy hair. With his old pal Jeffrey (George Harrison to you), he became drawn for a while to matters spiritual.

But now he has settled down to the role of a kind of musical labourer, as he seeks security and stability in the English working class ethics and manners. His speech has that assured authority of a saloon-bar man who divides the world into two groups of people - beer drinkers, and non-beer drinkers.

It may not be 100 per cent the real Eric Clapton, but

it's a good solid base to work from, and it makes life less complicated - although, even here, I suspect that taking a stand on one lifestyle is not always easy.

While Eric enjoys talking about football to strangers in the bar, the commitment to being English and working class requires entrenched, conservative attitudes.

A few years ago, at Birmingham during a gig, Eric made a few remarks that seemed to support Enoch Powell's view on repatriation. As a direct result of this, Rock Against Racism was born. The left rose to fight what they feared might be popular support for the right.

But Eric is non-political and can hardly be called a racist. He has long idolised black music and musicians. Nevertheless, he seems to feel that unchecked immigration is still an issue, and it was one of the matters we touched on during a long conversation at Southampton's Polygon Hotel on Saturday afternoon. At first it seemed that Eric might well be lured off to a football match; but to start at the beginning…

The day dawned wet and miserable at Waterloo Station. Adrian Boot, hero of the Grateful Dead's Egyptian campaign, appeared clutching his trunk-load of cameras and reported that Jona Lewie of Stiff Tour fame was in the coffee shop.

Jona, a smartly dressed gent, clutching a piano accordion, was intrigued to hear of the expedition to see Clapton. He was on his way to a spot of promotion himself, down in Portsmouth, and remembered that the last time he saw Clapton was when Jona was in

Brett Marvin and the Thunderbolts. 'We did a tour with Derek & The Dominoes back in 1970. I remember Eric as a very thin man. He's bloomed out a bit since then.'

Andy Murray, one of Stiff's hierarchy, recalled that he had seen Eric play a secret holiday camp gig at Hayling Island. 'He played Layla for all these mums, dads and kids, and nobody seemed to recognise it, but when he played I Shot The Sheriff they knew it was a hit. He was going to play at another Butlin's but they had 7,000 applications for tickets. They panicked and cancelled the show.'

Another show that had to be cancelled more recently was the ill-fated Cream reunion, when Ginger Baker wanted to bring Eric and Jack Bruce together again at his polo club. Unfortunately, word was leaked to the national press and the polo fraternity also panicked, expecting an invasion of fans.

Andy laid Jona's album on me, apologised for blagging at 9.30 am on Waterloo Station, and we went our separate ways.

At Southampton, an hour away, football fans were already streaming into town for the afternoon's match. But at the Polygon Hotel, most of the Clapton camp were still sound asleep after a night of merriment following their gig at the Gaumont.

Roger Forrester, Eric's manager, was awake, however, bleary-eyed and clad in a dressing-gown, but keen that the long-delayed interview would take place.

'You know what I had to do to get Eric to agree to an

interview?' he demanded, ordering coffee from room service. 'I had to go on stage last night and announce the group. I was terrified. But once Eric gets an idea into his head he keeps on and on about it. So as I had to go on stage, he's GOT to do the interview.'

Not for another couple of hours was it deemed sensible to start knocking on Eric's door. He had not been to bed until 5 am, having been out dancing at the local discotheque. Rumour was that the local girls had not been impressed by Eric's John Travolta-style routine, and refused to join him on the floor, so in the end he had put a bandana round his head and danced alone.

It seemed odd that after years of avoiding publicity and trying to shake off his fame Eric was now approaching that state known to many a rock star in their 30s, when the younger generation fails to recognise them.

It seemed the height of irony when two girls sitting in the hotel bar (where we eventually found Eric, surrounded by football fans) revealed they had not the faintest idea who he was. Their favourite band was Showaddywaddy. They'd never heard of Cream or Bob Dylan, for that matter.

Eric has cut back on drinking considerably, but he felt that a glass or two of brandy might help ease us into the interview and was most affable and amenable. There was a moment when I tried to draw him away from the subject of football, and back to more pressing matters like Rock Against Racism, when he chided:

'Never mind what we were talking about. Now be courteous!'

What Eric had been saying about immigration was really just saloon-bar talk, and stemmed from a remark shouted at him the night before.

'Someone shouted out 'Enoch Powell' last night. And I had to spend half an hour after the gig explaining to Carl Radle that he wasn't the George Wallace of England. But I think Enoch is a prophet, see? His diplomacy is wrong, and he's got no idea how to present things. His ideas are right. You go to Heathrow any day, mate, and you'll see thousands of Indian people sitting there waiting to know whether or not they can come into the country. And you go to Jamaica and there's adverts on TV saying 'Come to lovely England', and pictures of double-decker buses.'

But didn't Eric think that Enoch was a racist?

'No, he's not,' said Eric firmly. 'I don't think he cares about colour of any kind. I think his whole idea is for us to stop being unfair to immigrants because it's getting out of order. A husband comes over, lives off the dole to try and save enough to bring his wife and six kids over. It's splitting up families, and I think the Government is being incredibly unfair to people abroad to lure them to the promised land where there is actually no work.

'The racist business starts when white guys see immigrants getting jobs and they're not. Enoch said six years ago, stop it, give 'em a grand, and tell 'em to go home.

'That whole thing about me talking about Enoch

88 **ERIC CLAPTON** slowhand

was that it occurred to me that he was the only bloke who was telling the truth, for the good of the country. I mean there's all sorts of things going on, smuggling routes... you can get as many people in this country as you like. And it's their families that suffer because they're left behind. I saw an Indian woman being grilled at Heathrow and it was the most anguishing scene you've ever seen in your life.'

'The woman has completely broken down, because she can hardly speak English, and she's come here expecting to be greeted by her husband and go to a new house. Next minute, she's back on the 'plane.'

Eric got a lot of stick for his previous outburst.

'Yeah, I did. But I don't mind. So did Enoch. They shoved him into Ireland. But he can do as much good there as he can anywhere. I believe he is a very religious man. And you can't be religious and racist at the same time. The two things are incompatible.'

But people might think that you are being racist yourself?

'Yeah, yeah. That was the original mistake.'

Meanwhile the dialogue between Eric and his new-found mates, the football fans, went something like this.

1st football fan: 'Wodger work - five nights a week?'

Eric: 'Nah, I couldn't 'andle that. I'm getting old, mate.

1st football fan: 'You must be, because when I was a kid you were still going.' (Shouts of laughter from all the company.)

Eric: 'THANK you.'

2nd football fan: 'Oh, yeah, was it with Cream or summink?'

Eric: 'All right, none of that...'

1st football fan: ''Ee was going afore that...'

Eric hastily changes the subject and looks across at the two rather beautiful girls sitting across the lounge. He leans towards me in conspiratorial fashion. ''Ere, go across and ask 'em how old they are.' What - those chicks? 'Yeah, the grumble. Well, it's company isn't it.'

At this point Roger Forrester appears in his manager's cap to borrow a couple of quid.

'Here you are, son, now go and enjoy yourself,' says Eric enjoying the situation, and producing a tenner.

'Oh Eric, I don't want all that, do I? That's very nice of you...'

The fans chuckle in good humour, throw back their beers, and - having failed to seduce Eric to the match - set off to watch Southampton beat Birmingham.

The two girls come over to join us for drinks, with bright, nervous smiles. They sense that somehow Eric is the centre of attraction, but reveal a charming ignorance.

'What do you work at?' asks one.

'Musician,' he responds, as if he were saying 'bricklayer' or 'industrial cleaning contractor'.

'What sort?'

'A rock 'n' roll musician.'

The girls persist with their probing questions. What was he doing here in Southampton, they'd like to know.

'I've come to do a gig here, haven't I,' says Eric. 'We played the Gaumont. Last night.' He begins to sound testy. We wonder who has been doing the promotion.

'Roger!' says Eric. 'He stands outside and offers people money to go in. I've been geeing Roger up, because he showed me last week's Melody Maker, and I wanted to know how much he paid to get us on the front page. How much was it, Chris?' Eric seems quite convinced that jiggery-pokery had been afoot.

'I mean, you don't like me,' he added.

I hastened to point out that quite a lot of water had rolled under the bridge. Past knocks had stemmed from duff gigs, but the band up in Glasgow the week before had been great.

'It was good fun, wasn't it?' said Eric quietly. 'Last night was a gas! Not many. Dear o Lor'. It steamed along. The band is incredibly tight.'

Was he happy working as a four-piece?

'It was the original deal. But it took us four years to get around to it. The original plan was that Carl would bring Dick Sims and Jamie Oldaker to Miami. Only they arrived late - being Tulsa people - and George Terry was already around, so he joined. It was a stitch-up if you ask me! No he hasn't quit. I just called him up and said that we were going out as a quartet. I was scared shitless of the idea, but it ended up him telling me not to worry. His attitude was fantastic.

'The first gig was a walkover, probably as good as any of the others. In fact it's easier with a four-piece. 'Cos when we had the girls and George, I was always looking from one side of the stage to the other to check out what was going on, and like two of the girls would be redundant a lot of the time, just sitting in chairs. That saps your energy and I don't think it was good for anybody. Wasn't good for them - or me.

'Trouble is - I can't fire people. Yvonne left because she wanted to pursue a solo career, and that was like saying 'Can I go?'

'The Dominoes was a four-piece band and I enjoyed that. It's the whole thing about having a Booker T-type feel. One guitar, keyboards, drums and bass. I have to work more, it's true, and that's what I really enjoy doing. Everybody has to work. We started out this tour trying too hard. Over-compensating. Now it's a lot more simplified. Booker T was your complete unit. You could add horns to it, and singers as you wanted.'

So Eric would stay with this band for a while?

'I think so. We've already done nine months' work…'

And how was he shaping up, physically?

'I'm tired, man, really tired. We went to a disco last night, and there were some really ugly birds there. There were about 20 bouncers to every fella. I spent most of my time chatting up the bouncers - so I wouldn't get hit! And there's no place to go to in London any more. The only club I go to is Rags. But that's a man's club. You never see women in there ever. They've got a pool table, backgammon and cards. You go in there and drink until everyone's fed up with it, or you play pool and that's it. There's no chance of pulling anything! London's no place to go. I never go there unless I can help it. Only on business.

'I was going to have a dance competition last night. I was all wound up and going to give it plenty, but no chance. None of the girls wanted to dance. I've always been a dancer. I've been a dancer all me life. Do you remember the Scene Club? You could just dance on your own there. And there was some place in Archer Street, the only one in England they called a discotheque.'

Eric was with the right label (RSO) for discos. How did he feel about the fantastic success of his old manager from the days of Cream, Robert Stigwood?

'I saw him recently and he doesn't know what's going on. He's transcended it completely. He's got more money than he knows what to do with. Billionaire - I should think. And yet he's exactly the same. He's still the same great bloke. He's a GREAT bloke. All he cares about is maintaining friendships, because money can get in the way of that, rapidly. In business all he has to say is yey or nay.

'Sometimes he comes up with some great ideas, other times he just gives his consent. Sgt Pepper was one idea that died, though. It really died. He offered me a part in it. I was supposed to play a weather vane or something. Billy Preston ended up doing it.'

Eric, who recently re-signed to the Stigwood organisation, stipulated in his contract that he would NOT be offered any film scripts. Apparently his experience in Tommy was enough, although he is keen to complete his own film documentary of the Clapton band on the road.

He had seemingly fought shy of the media in recent years, rarely giving interviews, and those around him often complained vociferously of the treatment meted out to him in reviews and articles.

Australia was one place the Clapton camp vowed they would not return to again because of hounding by national newspaper reporters, who camped outside the door and ran stories about him and Patti Boyd. One paper had run a picure captioned 'Ex-drug addict'. But Eric seemed genuinely surprised at the heat this aroused in his friends and compatriots. For example, he wondered if I had been winding up Jamie Oldaker, who sprang to Eric's defence in last week's episode of the Clapton Saga.

'It sounded like he'd lost his temper. Did you wind him up or something? I didn't realise he cared so much. It's amazing, ennit?'

Had it been an accurate portrayal of how Eric felt about the press?

'Hmmm…' he thought for a moment. 'No… the press is fine. But I don't think the press ever gets anything right. Reporting-wise, I mean. I don't think anyone has ever pulled that off. I don't think it can be done. Do you?'

My response was to refer to the hypothetical accident and the four hypothetical witnesses who all give different accounts. I referred back to the early days of Eric's comeback, when one got the impression that he didn't want to project himself too much, and his playing seemed listless.

'Yeah, well, everyone likes to be lazy sometimes…'

The girls momentarily distracted Eric. Why was he talking to me all the time?

'Because I'm doing a bleeding interview,' explained EC.

One of Eric's happier memories of the past year was working with Bob Dylan on his historic European tour, and Eric's album title, Backless, was a kind of in-joke about working for Bob Dylan's back, as the master had a habit of turning round and giving a fairly serious stare if the band were not entirely pulling their weight, a technique he may have borrowed from Benny Goodman, the jazz clarinettist also noted for 'the ray'.

'It was an inspiration working for Bob. Sometimes he'd turn round and it would be like 'Okay, you're not listening' and he knew all the time if you were paying attention or not. He knew what everyone was doing behind him.

'The best gig we did was in Nuremburg. It was the place where Adolf used to hold the rallies. The place where he used to come out and stand on his podium was directly opposite us. It was a black doorway. And he'd come out to an incredible atmosphere. The atmosphere was there, again but this time it was for a Jewish songwriter. And Bob didn't even know.'

Eric had known and worked with Dylan over a number of years. What was he like as a…

Eric interrupted me, his attention again engaged by the girls.

'She doesn't even know who Bob Dylan, is, do you realise that? I do get on with Bob very well, though, I love him, he's a fantastic guy. And I still love The Band. My soul brother is Richard Manuel, who plays the piano.

'The first time I worked with Bob was when I was with John Mayall. He came to London, and liked John, who had made a record called Life Is Like a Slow Train Crawling Up a Hill, and Bob was very freaked out by this. After calling up the zoo and asking if he could have a giraffe delivered to his room, he called up John and we did a session at Chappell's in Bond Street. Tom Wilson was the producer and there was a huge entourage.

'Thousands of people were telling me, 'Don't play country style, play city, go electric, don't play acoustic'. It was all this. And Bob gets on the piano and starts playing. The next thing you know, there's nothing happening.

'And I said, 'what's happening, Where's he gone?' And he'd gone to Madrid.

'This was back in '65. It's never been a serious friendship. We just jive. It's like working with Muddy, you know. We don't talk seriously. That's forbidden. It's an unwritten law. You don't say anything like 'I've always liked your music'.

'I can't watch Muddy. It drains me completely. When he does that song I'm A Man, I have to scream. I didn't want Muddy on tour to begin with.'

This seemed an astonishing statement, but he

slowhand **ERIC CLAPTON** | **93**

explained: 'I thought it would be beyond my capabilities to follow Muddy. I just couldn't handle the idea of following Muddy on stage. Originally we tried to get the Paul Butterfield Band, because Paul and I are very much the same kind of characters. There's no big deal there, and he's a harp player. But at the last minute Paul couldn't get his band together.'

I thought Eric was playing more powerful guitar.

'Well I've GOT to. Coming on after Muddy Waters, you've gotta do something, and it's gotta be right. Nah, I don't practice, I get it from the band. That's where it comes from. They're the source.

'If I'm on my own in a room, who have I got to play for? I'll write a song maybe, if it's there to write. I like to play for other people. It's always for someone else. You don't do anything for your own pleasure, do you? There is a point where you've got something almost right, and you don't want to present it to anybody unless it's absolutely right. But, no, I'm not a perfectionist. Unskilled labour. Hard work. That's all it is.'

Did Eric feel a sense of disorientation afer his illness and cure from addiction?

'I was worried. I just didn't know where I was going. I didn't know whether I should carry on, or whether I should pack it in altogether.

'And then a song came along. It was Dear Lord, Give Me Strength. It just kept coming through, like a dream. It kept coming back to me. I thought if I didn't do something, then I would be letting people down. That gave me the strength to carry on being a musician.'

But there were practical considerations, too.

'I couldn't knock it on the head, anyway. Businesswise I was in breach, of contract, because I hadn't done anything for three years. My contract said I had to make at least two albums a year and go on the road. So I HAD to and I knew that. It was in the back of my mind as well. It was really a matter of loyalty and word of honour. Robert Stigwood would never have come down on me, but I had given my word, whether it was written on paper or a handshake. That was a strong factor in pulling me through, too. Now I'm enjoying playing and there's nothing in the way.'

What did he think of the audiences, and the kids who came to see him today?

'I don't take any notice. Do you know what I look at? The exit signs. I can just about see the kids coming in and going out. At one gig the kids started shouting at me, 'Duane All-man'.'

Eric began shouting at the top of his voice, causing the hotel fittings and fixtures to reverberate.

'Duane Allman!' he bellowed. 'Jack Bruce!' Eric shook his head.

'They actually stand up and shout. It's a roar. They don't even seem to realise that Duane has been dead for about four years. So I just showed them the back of my guitar and walked off, after doing my alloted time, of course.'

Does Eric feel that the past hangs over him like a cloud?

'It doesn't hang over me, I can handle it, but I feel

for the band. Christ almighty, this is the LONGEST I've ever been with a band. And if they can't show some kind of appreciation for them...

'I mean, Jack has got his own life to lead, and so have I, and there are three other people playing on stage with me that are going to get hurt by all this. That incenses me, it really does.' He paused to reflect.

'But then you don't always KNOW how can you tell what's going through that guy's mind, when he shouts for Duane Allman? He might be meaning well. He might be saying 'Great, do you remember Duane Allman?' But I mean the Cream, with Jack and Ginger, was ten years ago. And I've been back on the road, now, longer than I was off it. For four-and-a-half years.'

Eric insisted his 81-year-old grandmother knew more about the rock business than most kids. 'She can tell me exactly what position the record is in the chart. She's a great songwriter too and I'm going to do a couple of her songs. Rose, she's a born musician.

'Ahh, knock it on the 'ead, you're driving me round the bend.'

I thought for a second this was an abrupt termination of our interview but realised that Eric was addressing his remarks to Adrian Boot, who was beavering away with his flashgun. But Eric relented and requested a picture of himself dancing.

'Did you know,' he said, sounding like Michael Caine, 'that John Travolta couldn't dance before he made that movie?'

I hazarded that he looked like one of Devo.

'The best dancer in the world is Bob Marley,' said Clapton.

As far as Eric's current musical tastes go, his favourite is Elton John.

'I've been playing his album for the last three weeks. Every day. It's the greatest thing I've heard this year. It's gotta be the record of the year.'

One of the girls decided to ask a question we had all overlooked. 'What do you do in the group?' she asked sweetly.

'I play guitar and sing,' said Eric pleasantly.

'And the only person who asks me to do sessions these days,' he said, returning to the official interview, 'is George. And he's just finished a magnificent album but it won't be out until January because he's got held up on the cover. He probably can't make up his mind what to call it. He suggested that my next album should be called 'The Sound Of One Hand Clapton.' He's much happier and looser now. He's got a kid, as you know, and it's given him a new lease of life.'

Has Eric thought of starting a family?

'I've tried, mate, I've tried. The first couple of kids I ever started to have were aborted because it was a bit dicey. But not having a family doesn't concern me really because I'm still a road musician and I can see that going on forever. I'm a wanderer, a gypo. I get three days off, I go home and I have a row, with everybody. I wander about and complain about things. Get back on the road, and I'm as happy as a sandboy.'

That's good, I observed.

96 | **ERIC CLAPTON** slowhand

'It's NOT,' corrected Eric. 'No, it isn't, mate.'

Well, it was good for Eric Clapton fans surely?

'Well, I'm not one to put down roots, but Jamie has just got married again and he and his wife need to be close together, so he's got this incredible turmoil going on. He doesn't know whether to throw in the road and stick to a home life, or take her with him; and she doesn't like travelling. And I don't want that kind of problem.

'I've been on the road too long man, I can't give it up.'

And how much further did he feel he could stay, on the road?

'Until I drop, mate. 'Till I drop.'

Why had he always worked with American musicians, since the demise of Blind Faith back in '69?.

'Well, they're the best. I think they play better than most British musicians. The only two I've met who can come anywhere near Jamie and Can are Dave Markee and Henry Spinetti. I think they're fine. But they're session musicians, studio men. The Americans understand more about what has influenced me.

'It's like asking these girls about Howlin' Wolf. A blank, right? But the Americans, they know what I'm talking about, and with Carl it goes back to Louis Jordan. They know where it's all come from.'

Eric started off the whole British rock guitar hero thing. What does he think about his successors, and the development of the heavy rock guitar which could be traced from the Young birds, via Cream, Led Zeppelin etc. to the present wave of heavy metal?

'I think it's great,' said Eric, unexpectedly (I thought he might discover the whole movement). 'And the last person who is doing it is Brian May with Queen. I think that group is fantastic. And he is the only guitarist here who really knocks me out. Obviously, there are lots more, but it's the one who comes straight to my head, because I love the way he plays.'

But Eric's own guitar style over the years has remained free of flashy effects and all the inhuman sounds the technology can now unleash.

'I don't see how you can do all that and play at the same time. I mean you've got to stop and think about what button you're going to press, and then you stop playing. That only applies to me. Probably there are other people who can do three things at once. What comes out of the guitar is the most important thing. I can still blow myself away. I can still do that, you know.'

But for a long while Eric seemed to want to get away from the limelight as a lead guitar player with a unique, universal appeal.

'Yeah, I was fed up with being nominated all the time. It was just getting on my nerves. How can you live with that on your back? You can't. It's best just to be A Musician.

'Unskilled labour, that's what it's all about. And if you pull it out of the bag, all well and good. If you don't - it doesn't make any difference. If you are being WATCHED and EXAMINED, to see whether or not you can pull it off, and you blow it, Christ it comes down on you. It comes down hard, I tell you. People expect so much from you.'

What does Eric think of his old mates, guitar heroes of an earlier generation, now?

'Jeff Beck is my favourite. I think he's gotta be my favourite guitarist of all. He's mingling with the greats today, isn't he?

'And Peter Green, he came and stayed with me when he was having a really bad time, for about two weeks. And the first week, nothing. Not a word. And every now and then he'd complain 'Why are you doing this? Why are you listening to that? Why are you playing that way?' And then one sunny day I caught him outside in the garden, dancing his head off, and laughing. It was so good to see him enjoying himself at last. And then we had a play, and he had it all there, it was exactly the same. I know where he's at.

'He's got it there, and he's just decided he's not going to use it, until he feels like it.'

They were remarkable days in the sixties that produced the likes of Clapton, Hendrix, Beck and Green. What does he think of the British scene now? Is the talent still there?

'I don't think I'm the right person to ask. I'm looking at it from an older person's point of view. I'd be too critical.'

Mention of Sid Vicious reminded Eric of an unpleasant but salutory experience from his younger days: 'I once spent the night in jail in America. LA County jail. I was busted for being in a place where smoke was being used. It was with Buffalo Springfield and they all got done. Neil Young had a fit, because he's had a history of epilepsy. He may be cured now.

'But in jail we had to take all our clothes off and line up for mug shots, and then they hosed us down and sprayed us with insecticide and took our clothes away. While they're doing all this, Neil just went. 'Wh-o-o-a-!' and they took him out of the room, and it was the last I saw of him. I spent the night in a cell with three Black Panthers, and I had to convince them that I was a blues guitarist.

'When I look back, it was a good experience. I'll know never to get busted. No way. One night of that was hell. Because there was no word to the outside world. It's a good idea when they take young offenders to a prison and show them what it's like, because it's not like joining the army. And I had PINK boots on! And I had me frizzed-out hairstyle, and I was wearing all my psychedelic gear.

'They took all me bracelets and chains away from me and I got blue denims with LA County Jail written all over them. But they left me in the pink boots and threw me in the cell with three Black Panthers.

'It was like I was a punk, y'know? I just had to keep talking and tell them I was English and didn't really understand what was going on, but I played blues guitar and dug Willie Dixon, and Muddy Waters, and Bo Diddley and Chuck Berry. It worked. It cooled them out - just about.

'I think they had been in for about three or four years.

slowhand **ERIC CLAPTON** | **99**

Eventually I applied for bail. There was one guy there who had been applying for bail every day for seven years, but nobody had put the money up for him.'

What is the driving force that keeps a musician like Eric on the road after a lifetime in bands, despite all the hassles?

A deathly silence greeted this, and Eric signalled with his eyes towards the girls sitting across the room.

'Robbie Robertson is asked by Ronnie Hawkins to join The Band in The Last Waltz, and Robbie asks: 'How much does it pay?' And Ronnie says: ' It don't pay nuthin' but you get more pussy than Frank Sinatra'. And that's it, y'know. I play poker and I love winning money at poker, but I love women more.'

Isn't money a motive?

'No, no. I've earned a lot of money, but I've lost a lot, too. I've been frivolous, not generous. And Cream only broke even, you know. Most of the money we made from Cream went towards financing the Bee Gees,'

'We joined up with Robert (Stigwood), went out on the road for six months at a time and made an incredible amount of money which went straight back into the company so that he could bring the Bee Gees back from Australia, and start them. But it balanced out. It was all in the company and it was like a family deal and it still is.

'The last year has been very tough because Robert hasn't been putting himself about much, he's got so many things in the pot. I've watched people losing their jobs without even knowing why, RSO people who have been in the family for as long as I've been with the label. They've been told to clear their desks and be out by Monday. And they don't know why.

'My contract was up, and I wondered, should I stay with this lot if they're going to get this cold? But I did re-sign because I don't think there is anybody else that I trust or love as much as Robert. When the contract came up, he said: 'You can write your own ticket'. So I signed.

'But there were clauses in the contract. One was that I didn't appear in any film unless it was under my own name. But I wouldn't mind making a guest spot in a film, as long as it was under my own name. Like those old jazz films which had Cab Galloway appearing as himself, not playing a role.

'Next year I'll probably make another album, go to America and tour for two or three months. That's the plan so far. And then I'll probably have a good time off, maybe six or seven months.'

Would he start making model airplanes again?

'Ooch, no, not on your Nellie. That was only when I was really ill. That was the only thing that kept me alive. It was therapy. My eyes got so bad during that time, I ended up using magnifying glasses and old people's spectacles, just so I could paint the finest bits, like the eyes on a pilot.'

What's his view of the 'casualty' aspect of rock 'n' roll?

'A lot of people go down on the road, but you can't tell when it's going to happen. If a musician quits the road, it doesn't mean he ain't gonna get run over by a bus.

'Like when I had that accident right outside my house. I didn't know where I was for two weeks afterwards. I was in a Ferrari and had probably reached about 90 mph in a very short space of time, when a laundry van appeared. That was the last thing I can remember. All I know is I hit him and turned his van over. My skid marks were in a straight line and they found me with my head hanging through a side window. You only need to do that sort of thing once.'

After his rehabilitation from drugs, he seemed to allow excessive drinking to replace one stairway to oblivion with another. Now he seems much more careful.

'I don't get legless much any more. When I'm at home and I've got nothing to do, then I'll have a drink. If I get one over the eight, I only have to look at Jamie, Dickie or Carl and I can see the disapproval straight away. They are depending on me to keep my end up. If I blow it, why should they bother?'

Now Eric has the responsibility of being a band leader.

'I'm not a very good one yet, but I'm learning every day. I never wanted to be a leader, and I still don't really enjoy it. As you were saying earlier, I always worshipped The Band. That was because there was no apparent bandleader. It turned out there was one - Robbie Robertson. But he was very much behind the scenes.

'Carl is mostly our leader. He's The Rock. He's The Elder. If ever I'm in doubt about anything, he'll put me straight. I'm not talking about the running order at gigs. I mean he can be a philosophical guide towards what is happening in your life. He's got all the answers you need. But he's not the closest to me. We're all pretty close. Some of us drift away for a day or two, then come back.'

It was good to see EC back. Down in the lobby suitcases and bags began to pile up, and people began to ask each other who was in their room and who was ready to go.

Clapton was on the road once more, this time heading for Brighton, ready to play some guitar, sing a little and stomp with his friends. Let's hope we see him again soon.

'Well,' said Eric, 'you'll get a Christmas card from me this year. And I'll draw it myself.'

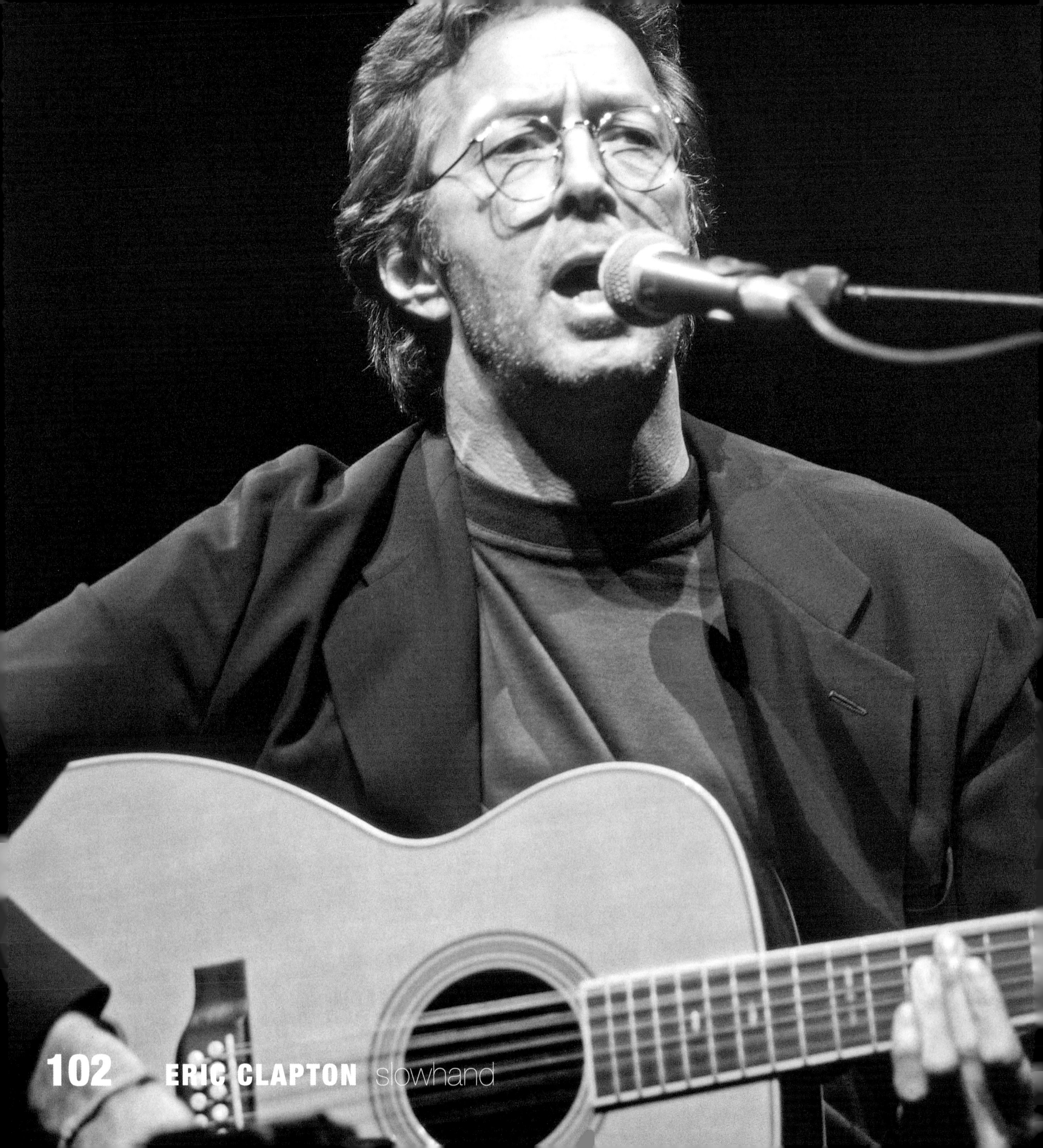

ERIC CLAPTON:
the solo artist

(ROBERT SANDALL, Q, JANRUARY 1990)

Quietly reinvented, curiously coiffeured, steadfastly single, and with an unprecedented 18 sold-out shows at the Albert Hall, Eric Clapton enters the 90s more a battered monument to popular culture than an unrepentant monster of rock 'n' roll. But there's a price. 'My personal life is chaotic,' he tells Robert Sandall. 'It's like something out of Fellini...'

The first thing you notice about Eric Clapton is his size. In accordance with one of the stranger unwritten laws of rock legendarines, he's smaller in person than his stage, screen and album cover appearances lead you to anticipate. Neither that fashionably roomy Italian leather jacket, not those viciously painted cowboy boots can make up for the fact that Eric is about four inches shorter than expected and looks, in T-shirt terms, on the small side of medium.

The second thing that strikes you is the unaffectedly friendly and relaxed way in which this shy, bearded guitar hero who only gives 'rare' interviews, guards his privacy, lives alone and so on, greets a complete stranger. Eric by name and Eric by nature, Clapton comes on as a convincingly regular bloke. The hand shake is firm, the grin is easy, the eye contact immediate and regularly maintained. Whatever you want to talk about is fine by him, he says, lighting the first of several Rothmans and sinking back into the sofa at his management's offices near Regent's Park. This modestly proportioned, private man and his gigantic public reputation seem more than comfortable with each other. At the age of 44, Eric Clapton, you feel, has learned to quite enjoy being a legend. He's certainly had enough practice at it just recently. A South Bank Show all to himself in 1987; a special 'Silver Clef' trophy from the BPI in 1988 for being legendary for so long; an American 'Elvis' award early this year in the 'Best Guitarist' category; a half-hour of mellow self-celebration with Sue Lawley on Desert Island Discs this summer. Try as the tabloids still do to portray him as a foul-mouthed philandering reprobate, Clapton today is more widely perceived as a monument of popular culture than as a monster of rock 'n' roll. And that, give or take an 'I never really wanted to be famous', evidently suits him as well as the elegantly floppy hairdo and the expensively baggy clothes.

Far and away the oddest thing about him, and the one point at which his behaviour seems out of step with the informal protocol observed by rock legends the world over, is his attitude to live performance. Clapton can't leave it alone. For most major artists now, tours follow albums as slowly and predictably as night follows day.

But for Clapton, touring isn't a promotional necessity to be conducted on a three or four yearly cycle; it's a personal need which drives him out on to the road for months at a time every year and has brought him back to the Albert Hall every January now since 1987. Next year's stint - an unprecedented 18 nights - will be different: there is the new album, Journeyman, to support. There will be three shows of pure blues with guests Buddy Guy and Robert Cray. There will be a Special Event on the last three nights. But these,

apparently, are beside the point: he's there because he's there.

'I'm a very habitual person, and I like nothing more in my life than to have a kind of routine, even if it's only a yearly project at the Albert Hall. I don't see any reason for it to end. To me it's like setting up a new proms. Because, yes, I do tend towards delusions of grandeur. It's a failing of most musicians, I find. And next year's had to be a mammoth production. It started after the nine shows we did there last year, when I said to Michael Kamen, who I worked with on the scores of Edge Of Darkness and Lethal Weapon 2, Would you write me a concerto? I thought it would be nice to have a concerto, not just for guitar, but specifically for my guitar, composed around the way I play.'

Strange to relate, however, Kamen is composing this hour-long, three-part opus for blues guitar on a piano, with Clapton in close attendance, 'saying, 'Oh, I can't do that', or, 'Look, I can bend five semitones but I can't bend six'. Unable to read music, Clapton will have to learn his part by ear. The adagio and allegro must be memorised, but he does get to make up the best part himself.

'It's up to me to write the second movement. Are you familiar with the Rodriguez guitar concerto? Well, you must have heard the second movement, that's where all the heavy melodies are. It's very slow and passionate.'

Slow and passionate with grandiose classical overtones is how Clapton prefers his music nowadays, as anybody who heard him choosing Puccini, Prince's Purple Rain and Bizet for company on his Desert Island will remember. More attentive listeners to that programme may also have noticed Clapton's puzzling lack of interest in the guitar which – Sue Lawley had almost to remind him – he might like to take with him as his one luxury item. (A Ferrari and an Armani suit were the items which sprang to his mind.)

Clapton's explanation for this omission is typical of the man himself: straightforward and direct in manner, a shade eccentric in substance.

'I just don't find it very inspiring to play the guitar on my own. Playing the guitar is a very sacred experience, and I feel kind of lonely doing it with no-one around. Music's got to be a shared experience and if I don't play onstage or on tour I don't play at all. It's my only way of disciplining myself. I never play at home. I don't have the necessary self-control and discipline to sit down and practise. Which is perhaps just as well because if I did I would probably develop a style which is totally unsuited to live music and quite alien to an improvised situation. As a matter of fact I haven't played properly now for almost a month and a half.'

Could this laissez-faire approach to technique have given rise to the curiously uncomplimentary nickname, 'Slowhand'?

'No. That was a joke on my surname: slow hand clap-ton. The thing with my technique is that I have to re-learn it over and over again in the presence of other musicians. That's why I always make sure that the band and I have got a good long stretch of rehearsals. Because I'm a lazy bastard and I think it's very important for me with my personality that I walk into a rehearsal room with the least amount to offer. I have to work twice as hard. The other guys will come in hot from doing a session the day before and I'll be all over the place. It's a challenge for me to climb back up again.'

This picture of our senior axeman 'reinventing himself' in the presence of his hired hands is confirmed by Clapton's accounts of his live performances. While most guitar solos today are portion-controlled affairs, as carefully planned in advance as concert ticket prices, his, he insists, are in the lap of the gods.

'For the most part I can't even remember what I played the night before, so I make it up as I go along. Mark Knopfler is a stickler for detail and he has to play his solos exactly the same every night as signals for the band. But I use the song as a launch pad for going off on a groove. The songs aren't as important to me as the grooves I get out of them. You know how we used to do I Shot The Sheriff after Crossroads and White Room, as the third song in every set? Well, the reason for its being there was to provide a platform for me to gauge the audience and the band and myself, so that everyone will know whether it's gonna be a good night or not. If it's a good solo it's gonna be OK. If not, it'll be a struggle.

'I don't dry up. Not completely. I can usually fool an audience. I mean, I can play an adequate solo anytime, but what I try to do is to put myself into a state of mind where I empty myself of all ideas and let something develop. It's like rolling the dice. You don't know what will happen. And if it doesn't work I'll have to come back to it and start again in the next number, and so on all night. Because for me it's not just a case of going on and doing a show, it's got to be better than the night before, and if it's not, everyone comes off disappointed. The band always knows. They give me a bollocking if I'm not pulling my weight. I wouldn't work with anyone who didn't. And that's one of the reasons I think I can sell out the Albert Hall for so many nights. Because people know it can go either way.'

Part of the key to Clapton's present success - and presumably also his occasional lack of it - is his present band. In the past he has worked with some great and famous names, Jack Bruce, Ginger Baker, Steve Winwood, Duane Allman and Ry Cooder to name but a few. But these have all tended to be unstable, provisional alliances. Clapton claims now that he was 'always playing underneath what I was capable of. I wasn't really inspired by any of them. Not even with Cream.' His current line-up is the best ever, he says, and it's about to become the longest-serving ever, too. Interestingly enough, it's also the one whose recruitment has had the least to do with him.

'It started with that abortive attempt to put out Behind The Sun in 1985. We (producer Phil Collins and himself) had it sent back to us by the record company because they said there wasn't a commercial song on

ERIC CLAPTON slowhand

the album. Now, I never wanted hits. I never wanted to have to deal with that. But faced with the prospect that this record would be a flop, that it would be hard to promote and that it was self-indulgent, I agreed to re-record a third of it. So Warners sent me some Jerry Williams song which I really loved and off I went to Los Angeles. There in the studio I met Greg Phillinganes and Nathan East. They'd been hired to play on the songs by the president of Warner Brothers, Lenny Waronker. I thought they were great. That's why I like this company after all the struggles we've been through, because all the senior executives, like Lenny, Ted Templeman and Russ Titelman (producer of Journeyman) are experienced ex-record producers.'

The band has since expanded to include drummer Steve Ferrone and percussionist Steve Clarke. They are an informal unit but their loyalty, according to Clapton, is absolute. Well, nearly absolute. 'Michael Jackson beats me with Greg. But now, you see, he left me to play Michael Jackson's world tour and he ended up being unhappy because there wasn't that much for him to do. It was a very tightly scripted show with a lot of machinery and programming involved, whereas with me Greg gets a lot of freedom. So does any musician if he's worth his salt. They can all write their own parts. I treat them well. And they know I can deliver the goods live.'

Perhaps it's down to his feelings about playing with the band; maybe it's response to all the media garlands and awards ballyhoo, but this year's Eric is far more bullish about himself and his music than the man who told Q three years ago that he 'sold himself a long time ago' and 'to make life easy.' Indeed the new album sounds like the work of a far more energetic and committed performer than the adult-oriented-rocker who coasted through the commercially massive, but dull, August.

When reminded that he had talked, at the time of August's release in 1986, of the 'dynamism you lose when you turn 30,' Clapton cheerfully and emphatically 'must contradict that statement.' He talks instead now of 'the wealth of experience' he can draw on. Of 'something' having happened to him since he turned 40. 'I think also that I'm lucky in that I've allowed myself to be led astray musically over the years. Muddy (his hero) Waters' problem was that he only had his own songs to do. He didn't let himself get involved in country music or reggae the way I have. Muddy had nowhere else to go.'

He continues in this upbeat vein praising what he sees as democratic improvements in the music scene around him, singling out the rise of African and other world musics as a particularly good thing.

'This stuff was around back in the 1960s, but if you listened to esoteric music then you were part of an exclusive club or an occultist sect. There was a lot of elitist thinking back in the 60s. For me to be a blues and R&B fan was like being a junkie. It had the same exclusivity attached to it. Now you can turn on the TV and it's normal to see Salif Keita or singers from

Bulgaria. And they're not being promoted in any way. You listen to these things next to each other and you can't say one is better than another. It's much healthier.'

These sunny observations all suggest that Clapton is, in himself, a happier man these days. Yet he still lives in glorious, high-security isolation down in Surrey. And one of the most eligible bachelors in rock talks publicly (and most recently on the South Bank Show tribute to Jimi Hendrix) about the loneliness that being a bit of a genius can bring. But what may once have been a painful predicament now seems to have been assimilated, almost as if it adds mysterious polish to the legend.

'My dedication to my music has driven everyone away. I don't particularly like it but I don't see a way round it. I've had girlfriends but I always end up on my own. I used to find that lonesome image very attractive, very bluesy, but now I'm stuck with it whether I like it or not.'

And what does that image conceal?

'An isolated, cold, rather intimidating, generally selfish person to be around. That's what my occupation has done to me. But given a choice I wouldn't have it any other way. I wouldn't want to be a happy family man, semi-retired, running a music publishing business with a photo album of Me and the Yardbirds and Me and John Mayall. I'd rather be doing this. The loneliest thing is when I come up to town to have dinner with people for a couple of hours, then get back in the car and drive home again. But I'll go out and create all

kinds of personal dramas to keep myself amused. My personal life now is chaotic. It should be filmed. It's like something out of Fellini: two or three different things going on that almost clash. But I dunno, I quite enjoy it.'

He doesn't, he admits, particularly enjoy being separated from his three-year-old son Connor - the product of a temporary relationship with an Italian actress and photographer Lori Del Santo. Mother and child are both now back in Milan and – outwardly at any rate – Clapton accepts this with the same stoicism that he treats his single status. Some suggest, however, that Clapton's currently lean and hungry look is not the result of a hectic year's live work but of his worries over his son's upbringing, that he is, in fact, looking not so much trim and healthy as thin and haggard. Reticent on this point, Clapton will only acknowledge that the way he lives now 'has more rewards than drawbacks.' And the new slimline appearance? A reflection perhaps of the fact that he is now permanently and completely off the booze after lapsing back into alcoholism two years ago.

'I was enjoying life as a social drinker for a while. But having a drink now and again led to having a drink all the time. I can't exercise any control over it. And one day I found myself drinking on my own at home, up to the old level, and it scared the life out of me. I was sober for two years, then drank for another two years and now it's been two years sober again. It takes a while to enjoy it but I find I like being sober now. I'm

slowhand **ERIC CLAPTON** | **111**

getting back on course.'

And what of his illustrious colleagues and neighbours? That much-fêted company who assemble in public to give and receive Brit awards, induct each other into America's Rock 'n' Roll Hall of Fame or pass around the statuettes at the 'Elvis' awards, held in New York back in May?

'I haven't seen any of those guys since that day. It's very difficult to be close to them. They're very blessed people and to be in their company warms my heart. We go, 'Oh, we were there in 1967, weren't we?' But although you sort of love them, you never see them. I mean, I see George (Harrison) and I see Pete (Townshend), but I know they're going through the same sort of lonely shit that I am. We never admit it to each other, of course. We all play that game.'

Surely he must see a lot of his close neighbour and musical collaborator Phil Collins? 'I don't see him very much at all, actually. He's a lot like me in that he keeps to himself. He lives about ten miles away but if we do meet socially we don't know what to do. We're so work-oriented that we find it almost impossible to just sit and talk.'

Work, Clapton says, is now his 'fun'. Italian designer clothes are 'my only vice'. Outdoor leisure pursuits have been gradually moved to the back-burner. The locals around his tiny village near Guildford report a lack of interest lately in the fly-fishing at which he is so expert. The Eric Clapton charity cricket XI - featuring Bill Wyman, the brothers Kemp from Spandau Ballet and a few real cricketers as well - has also been less active this summer. 'I'm never at home for more than two weeks at a time.'

Accompanying this mixture of restlessness and industriousness is a renewal of his old missionary zeal to spread the word about the blues. It's written all over the Journeyman album - his bluesiest for years - and it enters his conversation at regular intervals in the form of lengthy orations that make you wonder if some of those South Bank Show-style interviews might not have turned the man's head.

'I still feel protective towards the blues. It's a maligned art form and I get angry when I feel people are taking it too lightly. I go back to the blues because of its rawness. It's got more energy and vitality than anything I can think of. And you know black music is very deceptive. On the surface it looks like it's moving forward the whole time, but the bass lines and the vocal lines stay more or less exactly the same. If you take a line of Bobby Brown's and compare it to Bobby Bland you'll find there's not a lot of difference between them and what James Brown was doing 30 years ago. It's elaborated and addressed differently but the beat isn't that different. And most musicians who've been around will accept that the blues is the bottom line. It's always given me more out of life than sex, booze or any kick you can think of.

'I set myself a lofty set of principles at a very young age. It was very instinctive and very serious. And a lot of people doing it back in the 60s didn't, sad to say, have that kind of commitment. I was very dogmatic and if you hadn't heard of the people I liked, like Freddie King and Muddy, then I wouldn't talk to you. But it is an art form. And if you can see it that way and take it that seriously then you will get something out of it. If you don't, it will use you up.'

The guitarist who shares this lofty commitment to the blues and whom Clapton most admires nowadays is Robert Cray. Cray plays on some tracks on the Journeyman album and just having him around in the studio, Clapton reckons, had a decisive influence on the final shape of the record.

'The great thing about players as good as Robert is that when they're around you play to the top of your capability straight away. Like when he came in to do the solo on Old Love, I had the worst 'flu imaginable, but it was just like if Duane (Allman) or Jimi were there. You've got to do it. There's no rhubarb, no fucking around, you count it off and you play. There's nowhere to hide.

'We had a couple of days when we were dying to play and record something but we couldn't think of the right vehicle. We were both so keyed up it was like taking too much coke or something, you have to let it go. So we ended up playing Hound Dog and that slow blues on side two, Before You Accuse Me. We never really meant for those to go on the record, we were just soaking the energy up.'

Clapton is justifiably proud of this album. He says it's the only one he's ever made that he has carried on listening to after he finished the recording.

Defender of the blues, composer of concertos, rock prommer; Clapton is an ardent traditionalist these days, a small 'c' conservative whose continuing pre-eminence in his field combined with his readiness to perform for uncontroversially Good Causes, such as the Prince's Trust and Amnesty International, must make him a strong candidate for a knighthood. (Only last year Prince Charles presented him with, yes, another award, to mark his 25 years in the music business.) And although Clapton is dismissively modest about his vast accumulation of such honours - 'it's nice to get a pat on the back' - you sense that they actually mean a lot to him.

It is possible that they provide him with a more solid identity than any he can derive from his 'chaotic' personal life. Maybe they appeal also to the side of him that loves formality, distance and has an old-fashioned hankering after Englishness.

'I am English. I don't fit anywhere else. I've considered going to live in Switzerland for tax reasons, and for the privacy, because I've had an unnecessary pasting in the tabloids over here in the past two years. Which is not only a bitter pill for me to swallow, but it's terrible for my grandmother, who's 83. But there's something about the English, the working, complaining ethic, this working-class attitude. I don't approve of it but it runs through my veins. And we did invent something, the English gentleman, which is really something to be proud of, I think. We've all got that sense of it, even if we're not born well. We all know when we're offending somebody and back off. No-one else has that. There are no French gentlemen. There are no American gentlemen. But the great thing about English people is that they moan and groan a lot but they'll get on with it.'

He rises to leave, shakes hands, apologises for having another appointment. And, quite the model of English courtesy - and with just a hint of English evasiveness too - Eric Clapton is gone.